ALSO BY SUSAN COOPER

The Dark Is Rising Sequence

Over Sea, Under Stone

The Dark Is Rising

Greenwitch

The Grey King

Silver on the Tree

Ghost Hawk

Green Boy

Seaward

Victory

The Boggart

The Boggart and the Monster

King of Shadows

The Magician's Boy

The Silver Cow

THE BOGGART FIGHTS BACK

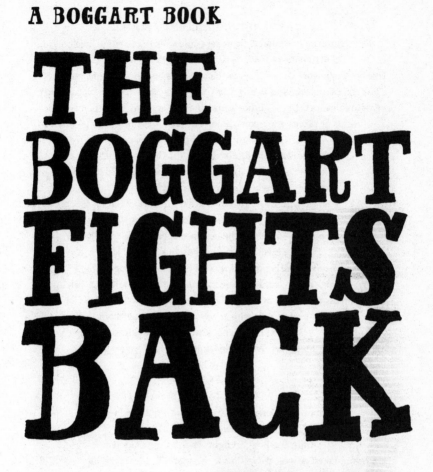

A BOGGART BOOK

THE BOGGART FIGHTS BACK

SUSAN COOPER

Margaret K. McElderry Books

New York London Toronto Sydney New Delhi

MARGARET K. McELDERRY BOOKS
An imprint of Simon & Schuster Children's Publishing Division
1230 Avenue of the Americas, New York, New York 10020

MARGARET K. McELDERRY BOOKS is a trademark of Simon & Schuster, Inc.
For information about special discounts for bulk purchases,
please contact Simon & Schuster Special Sales at 1-866-506-1949
or business@simonandschuster.com.
The Simon & Schuster Speakers Bureau can bring authors
to your live event. For more information or to book an event,
contact the Simon & Schuster Speakers Bureau at 1-866-248-3049
or visit our website at www.simonspeakers.com.
The text for this book was set in Palatino.
Manufactured in the United States of America
0118 FFG
First Edition
2 4 6 8 10 9 7 5 3 1

Library of Congress Cataloging-in-Publication Data
Names: Cooper, Susan, 1935– author.
Title: The Boggart fights back / Susan Cooper.
Description: First edition. | New York : Margaret K. McElderry Books, [2018] |
Series: The Boggart | Summary: Allie, Jay, the Boggart, and his cousin Nessie
strive to stop an American developer from destroying their home, even if that
means waking up deadly Old Magic creatures.
Identifiers: LCCN 2017017803 | ISBN 9781534406292 (hardcover) |
ISBN 9781534406315 (eBook)
Subjects: | CYAC: Magic—Fiction. | Americans—Scotland—Fiction. | Imaginary
creatures—Fiction. | Loch Ness monster—Fiction. | Scotland—Fiction. | BISAC:
JUVENILE FICTION / Fairy Tales & Folklore / General. | JUVENILE FICTION /
Fantasy & Magic. | JUVENILE FICTION / Action & Adventure / General.
Classification: LCC PZ7.C7878 Bt 2018 | DDC [Fic]—dc23
LC record available at https://lccn.loc.gov/2017017803

For
Cooper, Liam, Marina and Zoe
with love

THE BOGGART FIGHTS BACK

ONE

Out of the cold grey water of Loch Linnhe, the seals hauled themselves up onto the rocks, one by one. There they lay on the wet brown seaweed like large glistening pillows, flippers folded over their round chests, enjoying the sunshine. A herring gull swooped over them and away, watchful, keening its long mournful cry.

Inland, the mountains rose grey-green on the horizon, with cloud-shadows drifting over their slopes. Smoothed by time, the land was like a great hand holding the loch peacefully in its palm—and the seals lay there happily basking in its peace. The small waves lapped at the rocks around them.

And then noise broke in.

Up the loch from beyond the Isle of Lismore a motorboat came roaring, headed toward the rocks, white water foaming from its bow. There were three men in it, hunched down. Banking overhead again, the herring gull saw sunlight glint on the shiny bald head of the biggest of them. Then the shiny head jerked up and there was a shout, and the roaring engine gave a louder roar as the boat and its foamy wake suddenly slowed down.

One by one, the seals slipped into the water and disappeared. The boat swayed there alone.

"Hey—seals!" the big man called out, grinning. "That's a huge attraction, huge! We got a real live Scottish castle and real live Scottish seals! People are gonna just love that!"

"These are called the Seal Rocks, Mr. Trout," said the man at the helm quietly. The engine purred. The boat rocked on the echo of its own wake.

Big bald Mr. Trout stood up, beaming, clutching the windshield for balance, peering at the rocks. "And they're so close by! It'll be a perfect side trip from the hotel, perfect—come swim with the seals, folks! We'll give them snorkels and flippers! Guess they'll need full wet suits too, in this place." He gave a loud snicker.

The helmsman did not smile, but the third man in the boat, younger, laughed heartily. "Great idea!" he said. "Great!" Like Trout, he was wearing a black rain jacket with a large letter *T* printed in yellow on its back.

The helmsman said politely, "Seals are a protected species in Scotland, Mr. Trout."

Trout snorted, and waved his free hand. "So what? Nobody's going to shoot them, man! The seals'll love it too, believe me, I know about these things! Dolphins swim with people all the time at my Florida resort—everyone knows they enjoy it!"

"Absolutely true!" said the younger man firmly, and Trout smiled at him in approval. Then he turned away from the seals, facing the loch.

"And here's our biggest selling point—the castle!" He flung out his arm in a proud sweep toward the very small island beyond the Seal Rocks. It was not much more than a rock itself, but from its grassy back rose the neat square shape of the oldest and smallest castle in all of Scotland, Castle Keep. The water of the loch lapped peacefully around its edge, and beyond it the mountains rolled green and timeless into the distance.

"Perfect!" said the young man. He reached into an inside pocket for his cell phone and began taking pictures.

The helmsman waited in the rocking boat, silent. The engine thrummed.

"We're renting, but it'll be mine soon—just got to clear up a few legal details," Trout said. "Then I might make it look more the way people expect a castle to look—you know, battlements, all that stuff. On the shore, we got two hundred acres now, and there's nothing in the way—just a tacky little store. We're buying that, of course. Perfect! Plenty of room for the hotel and the condos, and all of it only ten minutes from the golf course! I'd buy that too, make it much, much better, a real Trout course—but it's municipal, belongs to the town."

The herring gull drifted high overhead, keening.

"But you got the castle, that's what matters!" the young man said. "I love it! You really hit the jackpot this time!"

"So I want you to get the website up just before we make the announcement, okay? No point in stirring up the screaming tree-huggers before we have to. And they'll be waiting, oh yes—all these fabulous developments I've done, but the lying agitators always try to make me the bad guy." Trout scowled for a moment, then brightened again. "Well, not this time ! We'll set up the website with all these beautiful pictures you're taking and then we'll announce—and I want a press conference that very day. Bring 'em all in by bus, buses from all over. Right?"

"Right!" said the young man fervently.

Mr. Trout swung round toward the man at the helm, flashing snowy white teeth in a broad suntanned face. "Okay, Dougal! Show him where the Trout Castle Resort's going to be! Let's go!"

He whacked him happily on the shoulder, ignoring the fact that the shoulder led to the hand on the boat's controls, and again the engine gave a sudden earsplitting roar. Hastily the helmsman calmed it, as the other two laughed, and the motorboat creamed away from the Seal Rocks, round the quiet unsuspecting island where Castle Keep stood.

And deep at the bottom of the loch, far below, a little twirling cloud of sand puffed up into the dark water, as something stirred. Something formless and ancient, which had been sleeping peacefully there in the sandy mud for years. One of the Old Things, a creature bound by no rules but those of the Wild Magic; a creature who might well have slept on for the rest of this century, if that sudden snarl of that boat's engine had not jolted it conscious again.

The Boggart was waking up, just in time.

TWO

Tom Cameron closed the trunk of his rented car, and looked out at the little wooden jetty on the shore of the loch. Then he looked past it, across the years and the memories, at grey Castle Keep rising from its green hummock in the great stretch of tranquil water beyond. The jetty hadn't been there when he was a boy, but his father's battered little dinghy, tied up to it now, looked just as tough and indomitable as it had thirty years before.

"That was my boat when I was your age," he said.

Jay said, "You had your *own boat*?"

"With a puny wee motor, though," Granda said. "Mine's better."

Jay stared at his father enviously. "You had your own boat *and* a motor."

Tom laughed, and settled himself in the car. "Don't get the idea that parents were softer then," he said. "Dad was a tough cookie. Until I was ten I didn't have a motor at all—he made me row."

Allie came running from the store with a bottle of Scottish spring water in her hand, and reached it in to him through the car window.

"Stay hydrated, Dad!" she said.

Tom Cameron grinned at her. "Thank you, doctor."

"And text us when you get to Edinburgh."

"He can't. I told you, we don't have reception here," Jay said, rolling his eyes. He was the practical twin.

Allie paused, deflated. "Shoot. I'd forgotten."

Their father started the engine. "I'll call you—on Granda's beautiful efficient old landline. And you use it too—call your mom. Often. You know how mad she was that she couldn't come."

"Working mothers!" said Jay, with an eye on his sister. "Huh!"

Allie took the bait instantly, satisfyingly. "It wasn't her fault!" she said indignantly. "She was just unlucky her meeting was in Ottawa and not here!" Then she saw her brother's grinning face, and she punched him.

"And you were lucky that I was luckier," Tom said. He winked at Granda, and started the engine. "Be good. I'll call you tonight. Bye, all!"

They waved as he drove off, along the track that would join the road snaking round Loch Linnhe toward the mountains.

Allie took her grandfather's hand. "Okay, Granda—now you're stuck with us, for two whole weeks," she said with satisfaction.

"Free labor," Angus Cameron said. "And ye'll likely be my defense against the dreaded visitors. The accents will confuse the heck out of them."

To the twins' eyes he was an older model of their father, Tom, this year more than ever: the same lean frame and watchful blue eyes, the same retreating curly hair—though on Granda, the curls were snowy white. For the past five years, since Grammie died, he had been visiting them each year in Toronto; this summer, to their delight, they were here instead.

Granda dropped Allie's hand and gave her ponytail a tug. "Back to work," he said, and he turned back toward the Port Appin Store, with its crowded windows full of everything from whisky to paper clips. Strictly speaking, Granda was a journalist; he had been briefly very famous, long before they were born, for taking the only unquestionably clear photograph of the Loch Ness Monster, still reproduced all over the world. But these days it was the store that earned him his living.

Out on the loch there was a brief roar from an engine, though it rapidly faded. They all looked but could see only the waves lapping at the shore, and the brooding shape of Castle Keep on its little island.

Granda sighed. "Speaking of visitors," he said.

Jay said hopefully, "Can we take your boat out?"

"Later. You can go with Portia. It's Monday—housekeeping day for the castle, until the season begins."

"Yay!" Allie said. "We get to go inside!"

"You get to vacuum, if she lets you," her grandfather said. "Come on, now."

They had met Portia; she was a masterful lady who arrived nearly every day to help Granda run the store and look after the castle, whose distant owners were seldom there. Until its summer tourist season began, the two of them were the keepers of the castle, protective and respectful.

Gulls swooped over the twins' heads as they walked back from the road, across the stretch of grass and stones that would be crowded wheel to wheel, soon, with the cars of holidaymakers arriving to admire Castle Keep. The most patient of these admirers would wait for hours to tour the inside of the castle, ferried over in small groups by one of the local schoolteachers who acted as guides, but many others came just to gaze and exclaim, and to buy snacks and souvenirs at Granda's store, as well as framed, signed copies of his famous photograph of the Monster. He was grateful, but always relieved when the summer ended and the stream of visitors became a trickle.

At the store door Jay paused, and turned for one more wistful look at the loch, trying to remember misty, haunting images from their only other visit to Scotland, when he and Allie had been five years old.

"The seals," he said. "Are the seals still there?"

Down on the bottom of the loch the Boggart paused, in his yawning way back into sleep. He looked up. Very, very dimly, against the faint glow that was all that this dark water would show him of the sunlight above its surface, he saw the flicker of a diving seal. For a moment he remembered the delight of diving like that, taking on that same shape, playing with the wild things.

And there was something else holding him back from sleep as well, something other than the seals; something else was calling to him. It was very faint, but he could sense it. Though there was nothing to see or hear, the call was reaching out to his ancient, magical, formless mind.

What was it?

Who was it?

* * *

In the store, Mozart's first Horn Concerto was playing softly out of the radio, over the groceries, and Portia was standing there motionless, looking worried. She was a brisk, compact person with short grey hair, and Granda had never seen her either motionless or worried before. He looked at her warily. She stood in the open doorway between the store and the kitchen of the house, still wearing her raincoat.

Allie beamed at her. "Morning, Portia!"

Portia was looking at Granda: an odd, strained look. "I'm making some tea," she said.

"That's nice," said Granda mildly.

"Dad took off to Edinburgh, for work," Jay said. "For two weeks!"

Portia paid him no attention. She held up a long white envelope. "I met the postman," she said.

"Portia," said Granda, "are ye all right?"

"There was a phone call for you too," Portia said. "Just now. I didn't realize you were out by the loch."

"Well, that's no problem," Granda said. "I'll ring them back."

"It was a man. He said it was about your selling the store."

There was a sudden silence. Even the music seemed to pause. The twins stared at her, and then at their grandfather.

"He sounded American." Portia's voice shook a little. "Angus, you aren't selling the store, are you?"

"Are ye joking?" said Granda. "Of course not."

She was still holding up the envelope. "And there's this. The man said there would be a letter."

"This is ridiculous," Granda said. He took the envelope, glanced at it briefly, and tore it in half.

"There have been several letters and several phone calls,"
he said. "And endless e-mails. From the Trout Corporation,
whoever they are. I said no the first time, but they keep on and
on. Someday they'll grasp the fact that when a Scot says no, he
means it."

"They want to buy the store?" Jay said.

"They want to buy this whole piece of coast and nae doubt
the castle, and build a resort for American tourists. Can you
believe it? Right here. But to my knowledge the castle's not for
sale and nor am I, so they've another think coming." Granda
dropped the pieces of envelope into a wastepaper basket.
"Portia, where's that tea?"

THREE

The sky was grey, but the air was warm. Portia steered the dinghy past the castle's tall, lichen-dappled stone walls and out across the loch toward the Seal Rocks.

"But only for five minutes," she said. "And if there's none there, we don't stay."

"Deal," Jay said. He sat in the bow, peering ahead. After this one diversion to look for the seals, they were on their way to help Portia give the castle its weekly cleaning, leaving Granda to man the store.

Allie was looking back at Castle Keep, rising from its small green island. "Those people couldn't really buy the castle, could they?" she said.

Portia shook her head firmly. "You heard what your grandfather said. Don't even think about it."

"Mmm," Allie said. She stared at the castle's towering grey walls. "It's just wonderful," she said. "But there's so few windows. And they're tiny. I'd forgotten how tiny they are."

"They kept out arrows and they kept out the wind," Portia said. "If you'd lived through a Scottish winter in the fifteenth century, you'd have wanted tiny windows too." She slowed the outboard motor a little as the boat dipped into a wave.

Allie was still looking back at Castle Keep, distracted only for a moment as a herring gull swooped over their wake. "Just think—all the time Dad was growing up here, he was looking at a *castle* out of his bedroom window. Amazing."

Portia said, "When your dad was a boy he used to help out the old clan chief over there, your grandad says, until he died. The MacDevon. And the last owner too, the lawyer—Mr. Mac, Angus calls him. He's dead too, now."

"And Mr. Mac had two nephews the same age as Dad, the guys who own it now," Jay said over his shoulder. He was half listening, but still focused on looking for seals. "He liked it when they came to visit, but he said they were no good in a boat."

"They still aren't," Portia said. She grinned. "You didn't hear me say that. Sam Johnson is a sweet man, but when he visits his castle once in a while, it's Angus has to take him over there. And the brother never comes at all. I don't think they're Scottish."

"Well, Dad sure is," Allie said.

Above their heads the gull keened its plaintive call, drifting, high up.

Jay said solemnly, "Our father is a diehard Canadian Scot."

"And Mom's family was part Scottish," Allie said. "Her dad, our Canadian grandad, he *owned* Castle Keep for a little while, did you know, Portia?"

"I heard," Portia said. "He inherited it when the MacDevon died, right? Because he had MacDevon blood."

"If only he'd kept it!" Allie said mournfully. "Mom loves it too. She was about our age when they came over to look."

"Very expensive, taking care of a place with an ocean in the way," Portia said. "If I inherited a house in Canada, I'd sell it in a flash."

Jay said to Allie, "Think positive. At least that was how Mom and Dad met."

"I know. That's what she always says." Allie sighed. Then she brightened. "And we have dual citizenship, Jay and me, you know that, Portia? Dad's had us doing Highland Dance since we were tiny. Competitions."

Portia speeded up again, between waves. "Do you win?"

"Sometimes," Allie said. "And Jay sings. Scottish ballads and stuff." She added, generously, "He's good."

"Do you sing too?"

"No way. I sound like a frog."

"She does," Jay said cheerfully. "And maybe I will too, when my voice breaks."

"What sort of ballads?" Portia said.

"A mix," Jay said. He thought for a moment, and then he began to sing. It was a clear true soprano voice, which he had taken great care never to reveal to his school friends on the hockey team, and it flowed out like dawning light over the water of the loch. Instinctively Portia slowed the engine down to a murmur.

"*Bonnie Charlie's noo awa,*" sang Jay,

> "*Safely o'er the friendly main,*
> *Mony a heart will break in twa*
> *Should he ne'er come back again.*"

His voice echoed out through the air—

—and through the water, and at the bottom of the loch, the

Boggart heard, and the last traces of his long sleepiness fell away.

"*Listen!*" he called joyously, in the silent Old Speech that only the Old Things can hear. "*Cuz! Listen!*"

But his cousin, the only other boggart in the Highlands and the Western Isles of Scotland, was still deep in the long sleep that had held them both there for years. Invisible to all but another boggart, he made long soft grunting noises into the peaty mud: *Hnnnnn . . . Hnnnnn . . .*

"*Wake up!*" shouted the Boggart.

And Jay's clear voice came lilting down again:

> "*Will ye no' come back again?*
> *Will ye no' come back again?*
> *Better lo'ed ye canna be*
> *Will ye no' come back again?*"

The Boggart's cousin stopped making his grunting noises, and he shifted uneasily.

The Boggart whirled in a fury, stirring up a cloud of mud, shouting at him. "*Wake up, wake up, you great gummock! Listen! You remember that song!*"

Up in the bow of the dinghy, Jay stopped.

"That's enough," he said.

"But it's beautiful," Portia said. "Just sing the chorus again."

"Go on," Allie said. "It might bring the seals."

"Oh, for—" said Jay. But he sang it once more.

> "*Will ye no' come back again?*
> *Will ye no' come back again?*

Better lo'ed ye canna be
Will ye no' come back again?"

And the Boggart's cousin, whose name was Nessie, heard the clear young voice and was suddenly wide awake. He blinked in the mud-misted water.

"It's the Stuart song!" he cried. *"The song for Prince Charlie!"*

"And that's a wee lad singing it, and he's a . . . he's a . . ." The Boggart strained to hear, but the voice had stopped. He tried desperately to call back whatever it was that he had sensed, but boggarts have very little memory. They are shape-shifters and jokesters; they very seldom remember the people they have encountered, or even loved. Only once in a while, once in a very great while.

Nessie felt a twinge of envy. *"Is it one of your MacDevon people?"* he said.

The Boggart gave up trying to remember. It was too hard.

"Let's be seals!" he said.

And up through the water of the loch they shot, changing as they went into the chunky streamlined shapes of the local seals—who were all at that moment away nearer the Isle of Lismore, fishing, and so did not witness the wakening return of the jokesters they had not seen for fifteen years.

The dinghy slowed as Portia brought it close to the Seal Rocks, glistening mounds that rose up higher than their heads, fringed with brown bladderwrack seaweed.

"Nobody here," she said. "You're out of luck, I'm afraid. But they'll be back—we'll come again in a day or so."

Allie was gazing out at the loch, hoping for even the briefest sight of the swimming doglike heads that had enchanted both her and Jay when they were five years old.

"It's the seals I remember best," she said wistfully.

And then from the bow Jay gave a shout, pointing, and out beyond the rocks they saw two gleaming dark heads poking out of the water, rising and falling in the small waves. One of them disappeared and rose again, then the other; it was as though they were playing, almost like a dance.

There was the faintest silvery quality to their skins, which would have told a real seal that these two were in fact shape-shifting boggarts, but Allie, Jay and Portia did not have the eyes of seals.

"There they are! Two of them!"

Allie laughed aloud, and even Portia was smiling. They stared out at the seals from the rocking boat, trying to guess where a head might next emerge. Then Allie gasped as she saw, right beside the bow of the boat, a surfacing head so close that she could see every detail of the doglike muzzle, the dripping whiskers and the big, round dark eyes.

And for an instant, the eyes were looking intently at Jay, who was facing in the other direction and could not look back.

"Jay!" Allie shrieked. But it was too late; the seal had disappeared under the water again.

The surface of the loch was empty, but for the lapping waves. The seals had gone.

"He was looking right at you and you didn't see!" Allie moaned. "He was so close!"

"Well, that's okay," Jay said. "We'll be back."

"*So* close!" Allie was still gazing out at the choppy grey water. She sighed.

And though of course she had no idea of this, the Boggart and Nessie were now even closer, hovering invisible and weightless alongside the dinghy as it hummed toward Castle Keep. They had stopped being seals. Shape-shifting took a lot of effort, whether they were putting themselves into the shape of a horse or a butterfly, and they were out of practice.

"*They're heading for the castle!*" the Boggart called happily, silently, to Nessie as the morning breeze blew through him.

"*Your people's castle,*" Nessie said mournfully. The castle of his own chosen clan, whom he too had haunted and tricked for centuries, was miles inland on Loch Ness, and had been blown up by hostile Englishmen in 1692.

"*And my clan's castle is yours too, you're my cuz!*" the Boggart said. "*Look, we're here!*"

With Nessie following, he hovered round Portia's head as she tied up the boat and followed the eager twins up the steep, perilous steps to the heavy door of Castle Keep. He waited restlessly for her to open the door. The insubstantial forms of boggarts can pass through almost any door or window that exists, but this door was fortified from long ago with broad strips of iron, the one substance whose ancient magic no Old Thing can pass.

The key was so big that Portia needed both her hands to turn it.

"There!" she said finally, pushing the big door open—and staggered for a moment, as the air around their heads whirled in the impatient passage of two unseen, unheard boggarts.

It was a comfortable castle, as medieval castles go. The

departed Mr. Mac had done his best to convert its echoing inner space into comfortable bedrooms and bathrooms, with thick, warm rugs muffling the cold stone floors of the linking corridors. For the past thirty years the castle had even had electricity. By its light, the twins happily investigated every room of the castle with Portia, dutifully dusting and vacuuming as they went.

At first the boggarts followed them, full of warm curiosity, but they had forgotten how noisy humans could be, and after a while they escaped to rooms where the howl of the vacuum cleaner was only a distant hum. Here they flittered about, once in a while capturing a vague memory of tricks played on tolerant clansmen centuries ago.

Allie gazed out of a slit-like window, across the loch to the purple hills of the Isle of Lismore, trying to take herself back in time. "Isn't it great? Imagine *living* here! All those generations of MacDevons . . . Can we come every day?"

"Your granda is hoping to take you fishing, I believe," Portia said, polishing a mirror with an old towel. "And hiking. He has bikes for you too."

Jay said, "And there's the seals."

"Well, almost every day," Allie said. "I just can't understand why those brothers who own it never come."

"No," said Portia sadly, "nor can your grandfather. He loves it much more than they do, if you ask me."

And in a while they were sitting at the big table in the welcoming modern kitchen, for a sustaining snack of chocolate cookies and mugs of tea. If the Boggart and Nessie had been in the room with them, the plate of cookies might puzzlingly have emptied sooner than it did, since boggarts have a great taste for chocolate and certain other treats, even though they need neither food nor drink at all. But the two boggarts had slowed down. They were tired, after the effort of hauling themselves not only back into consciousness, but into the shape of living creatures, swimming all the way across the loch to the castle.

"A wee nap?" Nessie suggested hopefully.

"Aye," the Boggart said. *"I'll show you where."*

And with Nessie following, he flittered along a hallway, up some broad stone steps and along an upper corridor, follow-ing an instinctive memory that he did not know he had—until he came to a big room with broad tables, several roomy arm-chairs, a big desk and a great many books.

He smiled.

All the walls of the room were lined with bookshelves and laden with centuries of books, carefully dusted by Portia not just today but every week, for this had been the library of Devon MacDevon, the last clan chief to live in Castle Keep. Even though the Johnson brothers seldom visited their castle, they vaguely respected the memory of the MacDevon and his vanished time, and had left the books where they were.

"This way," said the Boggart to Nessie, and he flittered into the library, and up to a space on a high shelf that he had occupied often, over the centuries, once for a very long time. There was more than enough room there for two boggart cousins, in a space between two blocks of stone, where three hundred years ago an absentminded mason had forgotten to put mortar, and an absent-minded carpenter had covered the forgetfulness with a shelf.

So Nessie and the Boggart flowed peacefully into the space, and went back to sleep.

FOUR

When Portia arrived at the store on her bicycle early next morning, Allie was standing at the kitchen stove, patiently stirring the contents of a large saucepan with a wooden spoon. On the other side of the kitchen the connecting door led into the store, but otherwise Granda's house was the shape of a normal house, with the kitchen and a living room downstairs, and two bedrooms, a bathroom and his office upstairs. The front bedroom, where Allie and Jay were sleeping, looked out at the loch and Castle Keep, the other at the green sweep of the hillside, dotted sometimes with grazing sheep.

Portia looked at Allie's saucepan. "Cooking?" she said.

"It's oatmeal."

"Porridge," Jay said. "Get it right. Porridge."

Allie said, "Made with those old-fashioned oats that Granda sells."

Jay said, taking dishes from the shelf, "Isn't it done yet?"

"Get a plate for Portia too." Allie went on stirring. "Dad taught us how, ages ago. With water, and salt. Granda brings oats over every time he comes to Toronto, he says no self-respecting Scot uses those little instant packages to make oatmeal."

"Porridge," said Portia in her very English voice. "That's what those self-respecting Scots call it, and so do I." She was from London, they knew: Granda had reported that Portia's Scottish partner, Julie, had brought her to live in Port Appin after they both retired as librarians, but that Julie had unexpectedly died. "So Portia was lonely and she looked for a job," he had said, "luckily for the store and me."

"The only trouble with porridge," Jay said, "is that it takes forever to cook."

"But is worth it."

"So long as there's brown sugar on top. And cream." He reached into the refrigerator for the jug. On the wall above his head, the long neck of the Loch Ness Monster curved up in Granda's famous long-ago photograph, just as it did in the framed copy in their house in Toronto.

And they were all three reaching for their spoons when they heard Granda's howl of rage from his office upstairs. At first they didn't know it was rage; they stared uneasily at one another for an instant, and then jumped to their feet to rescue him from whatever disaster had struck. But as they reached the stairs he was clattering down them, unharmed and cross, his white hair curling in a wild halo.

"Good morning!" said Portia.

"Damn these people!" Granda said gruffly. He stomped past them, heading for the door into the store.

"What people?" Jay said. "What's happening?"

"I've made porridge," Allie said.

Granda glanced at her and seemed to see everyone for the first time. "Uh," he said.

"It's still hot," Allie said. "I remembered the salt. Would you like some?"

"Look out there!" Granda stomped on through the door. "Look out there—and not a word to me!"

They followed him, and across all the displays in the store, out beyond the wide front window that faced the loch and the sky, they saw a gigantic black bus, emblazoned with the word TROUT in bright yellow capital letters. It drew slowly into the parking lot, where only two or three tourists had yet arrived today, and behind it came a long, sleek black car.

They all hurried after Granda as he made for the front door.

Portia said, "Mr. Johnson must have given them permission."

Granda snorted. "Wi'out asking me?"

"Well, you said he owned the parking lot," Portia said. "And they're . . . parking."

It was a beautiful morning, with strands of mist floating over the still surface of the loch. The sun glinted on the narrow windows of Castle Keep. The towering TROUT bus came gradually to a halt alongside the black car, and gave a loud, weary hiss as the driver switched off its engine.

A man in a battered raincoat emerged from the rear door of the car and hurried toward Granda, beaming. He had untidy long hair and a scraggly beard, with spectacles hanging round his neck.

"Angus!" he cried. "I've brought someone to meet you!"

"That's Sam Johnson!" Portia hissed to the twins.

Jay and Allie eyed the man doubtfully; he was about the same age as their father, and looked most unlike the owner of a castle. He waved to Portia, smiling, and shook Granda's hand warmly.

"Did you get my texts?" he said.

"No," Granda said. "My phone's a real phone."

"Oh," said Sam Johnson, taken aback. "Well, as you may have heard—"

And striding out of the car in his wake came William Trout, tall and wide, in his black rain jacket and pants to match. His gleaming bald head and broad white smile were heading straight for Granda.

"Mr. Cameron!" he cried. "William Trout—honored to meet you, sir! A privilege! Honored to meet the man who took that historic picture, which transformed the Scottish tourist industry!"

Granda looked at him coldly, ignoring the outstretched hand. "I'm no' sellin' you my store," he said, in a Scottish accent three times as broad as usual. "Or my land!"

Mr. Trout's eyes narrowed a little, and his smile faded. He lowered his hand. He said, "We've made you an excellent offer, a really excellent offer. I can't believe you'd want to reject it— not for such an exciting project, a project that does so much for the Scottish people!"

"Well, this Scottish person rejected it when it first came," Granda said. "I said no, so just tell your people tae stop asking."

"Mr. Cameron, as everyone will tell you, my projects are all first class, highly successful, amazingly successful, and I am a persistent man," William Trout said, unmoved. "And I'm not about to let one person get in the way of a development that brings so much good to the area."

Granda shook his head. "I'll not let Cameron land lie under a resort hotel," he said. "Never!"

"'Never' is a word I don't listen to, Mr. Cameron," said William Trout. "Not me, oh no. I'm a man who makes things happen. Once we sit down together with our lawyers, I'm sure we can make a deal."

Granda was looking hard at Sam Johnson, who flinched a little.

"And is that what ye've done wi' the castle, Sam? Made a deal wi' this fellow to turn it into a hotel? Your good uncle must be revolvin' in his grave!"

"They're just renting the castle for the moment," said Sam Johnson defensively. "And their hotel's going to be here on the mainland."

Granda's blue eyes were still fixed on him, belligerent and accusing. "Your uncle didnae want you to sell the castle—he put it into a trust, did he not? He told me that, before he died."

"Uh," said Sam Johnson. "Uh, well—"

Mr. Trout said easily, "Just a legal formality, the trust—my lawyers are taking care of that." He swept his gaze away from Granda, and it brushed over Allie and Jay and landed on Portia, standing there listening in her jeans and sweater.

"Mrs. Cameron, yes?" Trout said, flashing his smile again. "And your grandchildren, I guess?"

"Certainly not," said Portia in a clear and extremely English voice. "I am Portia Clegg, and I work here."

The bus driver chuckled, looking down at them all from his lofty window, and turned the chuckle hastily into a cough. He had learned fast that if you worked for Mr. Trout, you didn't laugh when he made a mistake.

Sam Johnson was still gazing at Granda, like a very small boy asking for attention. "Angus," he said plaintively.

"You didnae tell me about all this," Granda said.

"I texted you. Twice."

Jay said, "Granda doesn't do texts."

"And anyway there's no reception here," Allie said.

Mr. Trout nodded. "That's unacceptable," he said. "We're putting up a cell tower for the resort."

Portia said, "Mr. Johnson, these are Mr. Cameron's grandchildren from Canada. Allie and Jay."

Sam Johnson was instantly smiling and grateful; he looked, Allie thought, like a struggling swimmer who had been thrown a life belt. "Allie and Jay!" he said. "Welcome to Scotland! And to Castle Keep!"

"We've been here before," Jay said.

Allie tried to cover the chill in his voice. "And it's a beautiful castle," she said.

"Thank you!" said Sam Johnson warmly. "I loved coming here when I was your age too, but now . . . well . . . I'm just taking Mr. Trout over there. Would you like to come?"

Jay said, "We were there yesterday. Vacuuming."

"So it's good and clean!" said Sam Johnson with a desperate little laugh.

"We'd love to come," Allie said. "You aren't really going to sell it, are you? Please please don't."

As if she had never spoken, William Trout said, "Sorry, Sam—I want two of my people with me, so there's no room for the kids. They're in the bus—I'll give them a buzz."

"No," said Sam Johnson. He stood still, hands in his raincoat pockets.

"What?" said Mr. Trout. He looked at him as if he had just heard a sheep bark.

Sam Johnson said, "I'd like to show my castle just to you and these two kids today."

Allie thought she heard just the faintest stress on the word "my," and she watched with interest as Mr. Trout's expression changed from command to careful agreement. *He's not really in charge yet*, she thought.

"Sure," Mr. Trout said.

And out on the loch a motorboat came churning up to the little wooden jetty at the edge of the parking area. Out of long habit Granda moved onto the jetty to stave off a bump, and to take its bow line. Then he paused.

"Dougal MacLean!" he said. His voice held a naked mixture of astonishment and scorn. "Has he hired your boat? Are ye *workin'* for this man?"

The young man at the helm of the boat looked suddenly unhappy. "Good day, Angus. I'm—uh—it's just a ferry job, you know. Just a job."

Granda stood there holding the line, looking at him. He shook his head slowly, sadly.

"That's what we'll be doing for this area, Mr. Cameron!" cried William Trout, striding onto the jetty. "People love that I'll be creating many, many jobs, in a place where there aren't a lot, am I right? And to the man who photographed the Loch Ness Monster, Trout's publicity department can offer an absolutely terrific job! You're straight out of Central Casting, they'll love you!"

He smiled confidently at Granda, as he reached past him to take Dougal's outstretched arm for balance, and he stepped into the boat.

Granda said, "I've got a job. In my home. I've got a business, just like you, and I'm not about to give it up."

"Just like me?" Mr. Trout said. He smiled. "Really?"

Holding the line, steadying the boat, Granda looked at Sam Johnson, and shook his white head again.

"Get in, Sam," he said. "Take my twins with you, and bring 'em right back. They might as well make the best of their last chance to see the real Castle Keep."

Portia said in Allie's ear, "I'll make sure he eats some porridge."

Echoing through the upper corridor of Castle Keep, the voices rose and fell like a distant ocean. In his cozy space on the library shelf, the Boggart stirred.

The first voice was loud and assertive.

"So tell me, Sam, when were you last here?"

"It's been six months, I'm ashamed to say. I'm a busy man."

"I can relate to that. And your brother?"

"Eric never comes. He lives in New Zealand. Runs a fishing lodge."

There was a deep Trout chuckle. "Got his own castle, eh? I bet *he'll* be happy to sell me this one."

"Oh yes, he's all for it," Sam Johnson said. "But my uncle's trust . . . I don't know . . ."

"Money's more useful than an old place you never visit," said Mr. Trout, his voice suddenly crisp and businesslike. "My lawyers are working on it—they're in touch with yours. You'll like the price."

"Uh," Sam Johnson said.

"No more maintenance. Think of it. Your brother will be so happy!"

The Boggart, bored, paying no attention, tried to yawn himself back into sleep, but the voices were coming closer.

"What's in here?" demanded Mr. Trout. "Another bedroom?"

"This," said Jay's clear, cool voice, "was the private library of the last chieftain of the MacDevon clan."

The Boggart blinked himself awake. That was the voice of the boy from the Seal Rocks, the singing boy! He must be here, and perhaps the other as well: those two children who had somehow reminded him of something long ago and far away, which his wispy memory still could not find.

He flittered out from his space on the shelf and into the lofty room, leaving his sleeping cousin behind. He had always liked children; it was easy to tease them, and they were always slow to recognize that a boggart might be at work. They were not suspicious by nature. Dogs were the same, though cats were another matter. He looked down at Jay and Allie, as the group came into the library, and smiled to himself.

William Trout stood in the middle of the big room, among the massive tables and armchairs and the walls of shelves, looking round expansively. "Nice old place. Great atmosphere. I could take the whole thing to my new house, lock, stock and barrel." He grinned. "Got a new wife, you know. They always like to have their own mansion to decorate."

Allie said in alarm to Sam Johnson, "He couldn't do that, could he?"

Mr. Trout shouted with laughter. "I'm joking, honey! You can't always take the Trout seriously—only in business. Always in business, oh yes indeed. I'm famous for it—anybody will tell you that!"

He looked round the library again, thoughtfully. "This'd make a good headquarters, though, for now. Good place to set up all the plans, good place for meetings."

The Boggart looked at the expression on the faces of the twins, and felt a growing dislike for William Trout. He turned himself into a fly, and flew down and settled on the shining bald head. Trout reached up instinctively to brush him away. The Boggart flew up, gave a happy little buzz and settled again in the same place.

Trout swatted at him again. But the reactions of a Boggart are faster even than those of the sharp-eyed fly, faster than anything in this world, and he flew up and down again, several more times, while the twins and Sam Johnson watched in wonder as William Trout kept swatting at his own head.

And then suddenly the Boggart was bored, and switched back to his own invisible formless self. No boggart trick lasts for long. William Trout looked round at the ceiling uncertainly, his hand still raised.

"You got bugs in here!" he said. "Place needs fumigating!"

"Just a fly," Sam Johnson said mildly. "It seems to like the top of your head. Aftershave, perhaps?"

The twins looked with a sudden new interest at Mr. Trout's shining head, and Allie forgot the rule about not asking people personal questions.

"Do you shave your head, Mr. Trout?"

"Of course," said William Trout. He smiled. "I have incredible hair, but it looks ridiculous on camera if it's blowing around."

"You shave it every day?" said Jay.

"Does your dad shave every day?"

"Most days. But that's his face."

"Some men just shave their faces, some men shave their heads as well. Every day, in the shower." Mr. Trout bent closer to Jay's ear. "There's a special razor!" he said.

"Wow," Jay said.

"You can buy anything in this world, if you want it enough," William Trout said with satisfaction. "Remember that, young man. It's a good rule, and it's true."

The Boggart flittered invisibly round him, trying to think of something harmless but irritating. His trickery always began gently. He wafted himself outside the door, and made the insistent meow of a hungry cat.

The twins looked up in astonishment.

Mr. Trout frowned. "You didn't tell me there was a cat," he said. "It has to go. I'm allergic."

"Meow!" called the Boggart from the corridor, pleased. Then he did it again, even more heartrendingly. Twice.

"There's no cat in the castle," Sam Johnson said. He turned to Allie and Jay. "Is there?"

"We'll go see!" Allie said, and Jay hurried after her out of the door.

The Boggart flittered invisibly down the stairs, meowing as he went, trying not to giggle. He saw no reason to become a visible cat, since the sound was working so well. He led the twins to the kitchen.

Allie looked under the table. "Where *is* it?"

"And where did it come from? I haven't seen a cat at all,

not in the castle or anywhere else. Can cats swim?"

They stood still, listening. The room was silent, except for the soft murmur of the wind outside.

Without the satisfying sight of Mr. Trout's concerned face, the Boggart was bored with being a cat. He began touring the kitchen shelves, hoping to find a snack.

Jay and Allie searched the kitchen, baffled.

"It must have got out."

"The outside door's closed."

"But there's a window open—look."

Allie inspected the window above the kitchen sink, which had a gap of a few inches. "It sounded like a *big* cat," she said.

"Well, it's gone," said Jay.

Allie said, "This is really weird."

The Boggart flittered back to the library, passing Sam Johnson and Mr. Trout as they walked cautiously down the stairs.

"Wake up, cuz!" he called happily. *"We're going to have some real fun!"*

"We couldn't find that cat anywhere," Allie said to Sam Johnson as he came into the kitchen. "Must have been a stray."

"It was certainly very vocal," Sam Johnson said.

William Trout marched in after him, businesslike again. "Well, Sam," he said, "I think everything's just fine for us to go ahead. My development guy loves the place, and my people have the announcement all ready—we're all set for this tremendous addition to the Trout empire! You're okay with the rental terms, right, till the purchase goes through?"

"They're very satisfactory," Sam Johnson said.

Mr. Trout looked cautiously round the kitchen and headed for the outer door. "We'll add a clause about having no pets. Let's go, huh? Got to set up for the press conference tomorrow."

As they followed him out, Sam Johnson paused suddenly, looking round the high stone walls, so that Allie almost fell over his feet.

"That cat . . . ," he said.

Allie stared at him.

"It takes me back, seeing you two here," Sam Johnson said. "We were just about your age, the times I remember best. Tell me, do you and your brother play tricks on each other?"

Allie blinked. "Not really. Why?"

"My brother Eric was always playing tricks on me, here in the castle," Sam Johnson said. "And he always pretended he didn't, but he did, of course. That's the thing I remember best of all—the tricks drove me crazy, but it was fun. The odd thing was, he never ever did it at home."

FIVE

It was the sound of a bagpiper rehearsing that brought the Boggart across from the castle, the next day.

"Listen!" he called to Nessie, as the plaintive, unmistakable notes echoed over the water, and he shot out of the window into the cool air. And Nessie followed.

William Trout was about to hold his press conference. On the broad, rocky stretch of land that lay between the loch and the Port Appin Store, men from the Trout Corporation bus had spent half the morning setting up an enclosure of posts and yellow ribbons, like a kind of pretend corral. They trudged to and from the parking lot, carrying their loads, and Jay and Allie watched them from their bedroom window. The entrance to the corral was marked by two portable little gatehouses, set widely enough apart for the vans of television and sound equipment to come in. Three vans had arrived already.

Granda put his head round the bedroom door. "It's nearly time—you coming?" He had been sitting at his office computer for hours, looking for stories about all the other Trout Corporation resorts, and the battles over the ways they damaged local people's land and water and air.

Allie said, "Can I just check my e-mail?"

"Two minutes." Granda disappeared, with Jay following him, and Allie dived into his office. She was looking for a reply to the report she had sent to her mother the night before, and she found it.

Tell Granda to fight him! said the e-mail. *Condos and a hotel will pollute the loch and be a major environmental disaster! Aaargh! More later, with ammunition!!*

Allie grinned. Emily Cameron was a lawyer, with very strong feelings about protecting the earth and its climate; almost as soon as her twins could walk, she had been carrying them off to meetings protesting pipelines or promoting solar energy. The only thing that had held her back from coming to Scotland was a Canadian government hearing about the quality of the water in Lake Ontario.

Allie typed, *Go Mom!* and ran down the stairs.

Outside, more reporters and cameramen were joining the crowd, brought in by a second Trout Corporation bus from other parts of Scotland. Granda headed out of the house to join them, with Allie and Jay at his heels. The twins knew they wouldn't be allowed inside the bounds of the press conference, but there was nothing to stop them from listening.

Granda marched toward the gatehouses. As a freelance journalist he still wrote an occasional local story for the Glasgow *Herald*, but he was stopped at the entrance by an imposing Trout employee who was checking everyone's credentials.

"You're Mr. Cameron, from the store," said the man accusingly.

"Aye," said Granda. "And a paid-up member of the National

Union of Journalists. Here's my press card. Want to argue?"

The man examined both sides of the card with great care, and reluctantly handed it back. "Go on, then," he said. And Granda did, with a wave to Allie and Jay, who hovered outside the enclosure, hoping that he would actually ask Mr. Trout the ferocious questions he had been practicing at the breakfast table.

Then suddenly there was the spooky little discordant groan that is the sound of a set of bagpipes waking up, and along the coastal path came a procession led by a splendidly uniformed piper, playing "Highland Laddie" and followed by William Trout. Mr. Trout looked serious and important, though he was dressed in an oddly shaped tartan cap, green knee socks and a green kilt. Behind him, walking slowly and carefully in shoes not suitable for rocky paths, came several men in dark suits, and last of all came four men wearing Trout Corporation jackets and awkwardly carrying a large table covered by a green cloth.

And from the direction of Castle Keep, circling over their heads, unseen and unheard by anyone except a herring gull gliding far above, came the Boggart and Nessie, watchful, curious.

Mr. Trout stopped at a microphone waiting on a portable metal stand. "Hello, everyone," he said. "I'm very happy to be back in the homeland of my father's mother—whose tartan this is, of course." He indicated his kilt, smiling at them all expectantly.

The journalists looked at him in silence.

"Well," said William Trout, undeterred, "I'm here to unveil for you the most important boost that Scotland's economy will have this year, or even this decade. It's going to be a huge success, huge, as every one of my enterprises has always been, and it's going to transform this part of the Argyll coast! We're bringing revitalization, we're bringing hundreds of jobs and millions of pounds to this country! Ladies and gentlemen, the Trout Castle Resort!"

The four men had carefully set down their table beside him. Mr. Trout leaned sideways, and with a theatrical flourish he whisked away the green cloth that was covering it. Allie and Jay craned their necks, trying to see.

On the tabletop was a scale model of Loch Linnhe, Lismore Island, Castle Keep and the coast of Argyll, all green mountains and blue water. But from the modeled shoreline, at about the same point where they were all now standing, rose a large, elaborate, turreted hotel, with smaller buildings on either side. Groups of other buildings climbed up the hillside behind it, and down below, jutting into the loch near the castle's island, was a long jetty with dozens of little model boats on either side, like a marina.

There was no sign of Granda's store.

After a murmur of conversation, the journalists shifted closer, to take a look.

So did the Boggart and Nessie, flittering invisible overhead.

"Look, cuz, it's a wee copy of the loch! There's the castle!"

"But across from it, what's all that? It's another castle! An enemy castle, right next to ours!"

"As you'll see," said Mr. Trout into his microphone, "my world-famous architect friend Giorgio Tutti has designed another outstanding Trout hotel, this time in the style of an old Scottish mansion. I'm happy to say that he's here to answer any questions you may have!" He waved a hand at one of the men in suits, but went on talking. "Every room in the hotel will have a superb, unmatchable view of Castle Keep, and we have two hundred acres on which to build an Olympic-size pool, a spa, all the traditional Trout resort amenities. With four exceptionally landscaped areas of condominiums in the second stage of the development. World-class restaurants, prestigious stores—it'll be a magnet for the whole of Scotland!"

"It's that nasty man again!" the Boggart said, and instantly he became a fly and dived at William Trout's head, landing an inch or two from the green forage cap. He gave a little hop.

Mr. Trout swatted irritably at his head, and knocked off his cap.

"And what about the castle?" a reporter called out.

Jay said quietly to Allie, "And what about the seals?"

Mr. Trout said, "We are negotiating to buy Castle Keep, and we're renting it in the meantime." He reached up and ran his hand protectively over his gleaming head.

"Do you have full permission from the government?"

"Castle Keep is privately owned," said Mr. Trout. "For the resort, we've had great support from the council. I'm putting millions of pounds into this modern miracle, millions. Think what that does to the tax base! And six hundred jobs will be created!"

The Boggart dive-bombed his head again, touching down, bouncing up again, three times. Mr. Trout swatted at him furiously.

"Michael!" he hissed to a Trout underling. "Get rid of this fly!"

"What fly?" said the underling.

"Mr. Trout!" said Granda loudly. "Can ye tell us how you'd

stop a mammoth resort like this from polluting the loch and destroying the whole countryside? There's a major breeding ground for the grey seals not two hundred yards from the castle—have ye thought of that?"

Mr. Trout looked at him with recognition and dislike. "It's going to be environmentally perfect," he said. "I've built resorts all over the world, and I've had many, many environmental awards."

Granda said, "On this model of yours, is that a bridge going to Castle Keep?"

There was a stir in the crowd, as heads craned to peer at the model.

"A causeway," Mr. Trout said. "A stone causeway. There are causeways in many, many Scottish lochs, as I'm sure you know. For travel from the mainland. It's traditional, very traditional. We've done research. And of course all our hotel guests and condominium owners will need easy access to this beautiful castle."

Granda said, "*Traditionally*, castles were built on islands just tae stop anyone gettin' there from the mainland."

"This is part of the second stage of our plan, so nothing is yet cast in stone," Mr. Trout said. He gave a slightly strained smile. "Ha-ha," he added.

Nobody laughed.

A grey-haired woman reporter raised her hand, and Mr. Trout pointed at her in relief, though the relief did not last.

"What else do you propose to do to the castle?" the reporter demanded. "Are you making changes? Are you turning it into a hotel?"

"The castle and all other parts of stage two are still under consideration," Mr. Trout said curtly. He pointed at the model. "And our hotel is on the shore of the loch, as you can plainly see."

"How many rooms in the hotel, Mr. Trout?" called out a bearded young man with a microphone.

"Two hundred," said Mr. Trout proudly. "It's a luxury boutique hotel."

"Do you not think we have more than enough rooms in our existing hotels on this coast? They're very good."

"I'm sure they are," said William Trout. He smiled. "But last time I checked, none of them was a five-star hotel. *All* my hotels have a five-star rating."

"So you're catering to the very rich?" persisted the bearded young man.

"And bringing them to spend their money in Scotland," Mr. Trout said. "Anything wrong with that?"

"Yes!" whispered Allie in Jay's ear. "They'll roar around on jet-skis, and they'll scare away the seals!"

"Yes! And what about Granda's store?"

The bearded young man called out, "Mr. Trout, figures at your other resorts show that your rich visitors spend most of their money inside the resort. Is that not totally alien to the culture of farms and small villages in this area?"

William Trout looked out at the small crowd around him and smiled. "Ladies and gentlemen, I think we have a paid agitator among us," he said.

"I'm frae Channel Six News!" said the young man.

Trout ignored him. "Who else has a question?" he said.

Granda said very loudly indeed, "Mr. Trout, have ye not noticed that your architect's plan covers a home and an acre of land that ye dinna own?"

"In my long career in business, I've found that everything is negotiable," Mr. Trout said smoothly. "And Mr. Cameron, you are speaking now as a private person, and interrupting a press conference."

"I'm a member of the press but also a storekeeper," Granda said, "and my store's bang in the middle o' that ridiculous model of yours, and ye'll not have it!"

His voice rose angrily, and outside the enclosure Allie, to her surprise, heard herself call out, "That's right!"

Jay clutched her arm in support. He shouted, "No! You can't have it!"

Mr. Trout lost his temper. His broad face was suddenly red, and he thumped the fist of one hand into the palm of the other. "People will come here for the work of a brilliant world-famous architect! If that ramshackle store stays where it is, I'll take care our visitors don't have to look at it!"

"I don't want a great fancy hotel on my doorstep!" Granda roared. "And the folk here don't want you monkeying with Castle Keep!"

A great buzz of conversation began among the journalists, and some of them began to move toward Granda.

The Boggart called silently to Nessie, *"He's family with our young ones! And the uncouth man is an invader! It's a battle!"*

They had both seen so many battles in Scotland, over the centuries, against invaders, between clans. And they had always taken sides.

"Aye," said Nessie. *"And that enemy castle has to be kept out!"*

William Trout said into the microphone, "Well, ladies and gentlemen, come study the model. We'll switch now to individual interviews with those of us up here. For any of you." He turned and pointed deliberately at Granda. "Not you!" he said.

Granda looked at him, expressionless.

Trout turned back and spread his arms to his audience. "Come up here and talk to us. And if you want follow-up, I'll be back in a few days in my yacht, the *Trout Queen*. Now that's a sight to see too!"

His face tight and determined, Granda walked out past the two little gatehouses, ignoring friends and journalists trying to ask him questions, and the Boggart and Nessie wafted invisible after him.

A television cameraman near Jay and Allie, on the other side of the yellow ribbon, turned and pointed his camera at their faces, and the reporter beside him thrust a microphone toward them. Her long blond hair was draped round a gentle face, but there was a steely glint in her eye. "And who are you two?" she said.

"That's our grandfather!" Jay said. "He's a writer, and he's the one who took that famous picture of the Loch Ness Monster!"

"And that's his store!" said Allie, pointing.

The reporter blinked as she heard their accents. She said eagerly into her microphone, "And you're here from America to defend him against the Trout development?"

"Canada," they both said instantly, which seemed to please her even more.

SUSAN COOPER

But two large men wearing the black Trout Corporation jackets had appeared on either side of the twins. They had very short hair and very thick necks, and the quiet confidence of wrestlers.

"Sorry, kids," said one. "I must ask you to move away from the press conference."

"We're doing an individual interview," said the reporter indignantly. "Just like the man said!"

"Not with these two," said the second man, towering over her ominously. Like the first, he sounded American. He thrust out a massive hand at the cameraman. "And get that camera out of my face!"

The cameraman darted sideways and turned his lens on the large yellow *T* on the man's back.

"Very nice, Roger," said the reporter. She pulled out her cell phone, and her fingers began flying.

Allie and Jay ducked away, ignoring other hopeful questioners, to follow Granda back to the store. Still busily making notes, the blond reporter called after them, "Tell your grandad to get a lawyer!"

Granda said he already had a lawyer: a friend in Aberdeen, named Hamish, whom he had known since they were both at St. Andrew's University a very long time ago. "He came to stay for a weekend, a year or two ago. Portia was impressed."

"A nice down-to-earth man," Portia said. "And a very distinguished lawyer." She had watched the press conference from a distance, and when they all came back she had firmly locked the door of the store. Now she was making cheese-and-tomato

42

sandwiches for lunch, ignoring the sequence of hopeful jingling sounds from the store's door.

The Boggart and Nessie had flittered in with Granda, but she didn't know that.

Granda was sitting at the table in his favorite carved wooden chair, looking rather like an angry king on a throne. "I rang Hamish yesterday," he said. "He says that Trout can't touch the store or the land, if I don't want to sell. Not unless he gets something called a compulsory purchase order from the local council, which he won't."

"Are you sure?" said Allie nervously.

"Well, if he did, Hamish would appeal to the government, and Trout would have to stop his whole scheme for months. Aargh!" said Granda crossly, and added something in Gaelic, just to relieve his feelings.

"What did that mean?" Portia said.

"I'm not going to tell you," said Granda.

Jay said, "I really wish Dad had taught us the Gaelic. I do know one of those words you said. It meant—"

"Hush!" said Granda.

"Have some strengthening lunch, and a few of the evil treats your grandfather sells to young tourists," Portia said. She put a platter of cheese-and-tomato sandwiches in the middle of the table, and added several packages of potato crisps.

"*Cheese!*" breathed the Boggart to Nessie, as they floated overhead. His long invisible fingers reached down and extracted a sturdy slice of Cheddar cheese from the nearest sandwich. It disappeared in the instant that he touched it, but the top slice of bread wobbled a little.

Jay grabbed a sandwich. "But the lawyer can't stop them building the hotel?"

"No," Granda said. "Because the really bad news from this famous press conference is that clearly they've bought all the land next to me. It must be Trout who's bought Johnnie Robertson's land, that big farm along the shore. Johnnie hasn't been telling anybody who he sold it to, and now I understand why." He reached for a sandwich, bit into it hungrily and then surveyed it, chewing. "You forgot the cheese in this one, Portia," he said.

"I did?" said Portia. She stared at the sandwich, puzzled.

Allie said, "If he's got the land next to you, he can build the hotel, and everything else in that terrible model! And he's going to do awful things to the castle! This whole lovely place will be ruined!" Her voice quivered, and suddenly there were tears in her eyes.

Jay glanced at her with sympathy, as he helped himself to a bag of potato crisps. He felt just the same, even if he was less likely to pour it out in words. And the Boggart, feeling distress from both of them, forgot all about cheese. Though boggarts live only for themselves, though they have no care for the problems of most human beings, the impulse to help these people to whom he felt a mysterious connection washed over him like a rising tide.

He whirled invisibly round Nessie, so that Allie felt a breeze pass her head and put up a puzzled hand to her hair.

"*Back to the castle, cuz!*" he called. "*We have to guard it, to keep the enemy away!*"

SIX

After breakfast next morning, Granda was about to lead Jay and Allie up the hill behind the store, to photograph the reality of the view reproduced in William Trout's model, when the telephone rang.

He picked it up, and almost at once switched it to speakerphone, with his eyes on the twins. It was their father, Tom.

"Dad, what's happening?" demanded the voice out of the phone. "You were all over the local TV last night! And a shot of the twins, yelling, at that press conference. *William Trout*? The American developer? In Appin?"

"He's bought the Robertsons' farm," Granda said. "Nobody knew till it was too late."

"And he wants to build a *Trout resort hotel*? Right here on our doorstep? *And he's buying Castle Keep*?" Tom's voice rose even higher in disbelief.

"Looks like it," Granda said grimly. "Big business in action. I've been slow, but it has to be stopped. We have perfectly good hotels of our own—we don't need his. And as for the castle, don't get me started."

"Good," said Tom. "I'm coming back to help. Tonight."

Allie and Jay both cheered loudly, and they heard him laugh.

"But you're working," Granda said. "You have meetings. You crossed the Atlantic for them."

"This is more important," Tom Cameron said, and both twins recognized the note in his voice that showed there was no point at all in arguing. He also sounded more Scottish than usual.

So as their father went away to begin his drive back from Edinburgh to Appin, Jay and Allie and Granda climbed the steep grassy slope behind the store and took pictures of Castle Keep on its small green island, and the beautiful, still-untouched coast of Loch Linnhe. Above them rose the tree-capped summit of the hill. Granda gazed up at it.

"Up there, that's Johnnie's land, but he used to graze his sheep on my field," he said. "Do you remember? He had lambs last time you were here. Jay fed one from a bottle."

Allie said crossly, "I remember that, because I was a little wimp and wouldn't do it. Fancy being scared of a lamb."

"Well, it was butting at you. It was hungry," Jay said. Then he paused, looking up at the trees. "Granda, what are those?"

"What?" said Granda, squinting.

"On the trees. Stuff tied round the trunks."

They climbed higher, and found a plastic orange ribbon tied neatly round every tree at the outer edge. The trees were large, beautiful pines, wrapping the hilltop like a shawl.

"At home, those ribbons would be markers to show people where to start cutting trees down," Jay said.

Granda said, "That's what it means here, too." He added

something forceful in Gaelic, and this time nobody asked when it meant.

Allie said, "It's for his resort."

Jay said, "There were buildings on the hills, in his model."

"Well, of course," Granda said bitterly. "Just look at the view!"

"So they're already marking the trees to be cut down."

Jay looked at Allie, and Allie looked at Jay. Even though they were not identical twins, sometimes they thought as one. Each of them moved to a tree and carefully removed an orange marker.

Allie said, "If the trees aren't marked, nobody will know to cut them down. Right, Granda?"

"That's an excellent thought," Granda said. "It won't stop them for long, but it's worth a try. There's a bylaw here about littering—we're just clearing up the litter."

And together they began stripping the tree trunks and making a large collection of orange ribbons, which eventually found its way into the damp, smelly bag of rubbish at the bottom of the dustbin of the Port Appin General Store.

Tom Cameron drove into the parking lot that evening; the twins saw him from the kitchen and went running out to the car. After some enthusiastic hugs, their father pulled his suitcase out of the trunk with a determined gleam in his eye.

"Okay," he said. "Family into action. All the way from Edinburgh I've been thinking about this nightmare. A huge hotel, blocks of flats, a new sewage plant, hundreds of people and cars and delivery trucks, so many streetlights you'll never see the stars at night. The castle turned into a tacky theme park. No more seals—"

Jay said, "We haven't told Mom about the castle yet."

"Tell her!" said Tom. "Tell everybody! We've got to stop him!"

Allie said, "Was it really all right for you to leave your conference? You were looking forward to it."

"Sure it was," said her father. "I saw the people I wanted to see, I gave my paper last night and they liked it. Everything else I can do at a distance." He grinned at them. "Distance is what my job is about—you know that. Where's Granda?"

Tom Cameron was an astrophysicist at the University of Toronto, and the twins did know that he and his graduate students spent their time trying to trace the formation of distant galaxies, though it was nearly always impossible to understand anything they talked about.

"Granda's on the phone," Jay said. "Drumming up support."

"Good. Let's go give him some."

And Jay and Allie fell asleep that night to the continuing rumble from the kitchen of the voices of their father and grandfather, planning and discussing a campaign of meetings and letters, e-mails and petitions, to enlist everyone from local Appin neighbors to longtime friends of Granda's in the Scottish government. The voices rose and fell like gusting wind, and as sleep swallowed them up, each twin tried not to remember the orange ribbons of the Trout Corporation tied around the hilltop trees, and the chance that it might now be too late for any plans at all.

* * *

But it was indeed too late. Next morning, before they started breakfast, there was a deep rumbling sound out over the silent loch, and into the parking lot drove one of the Trout Corporation buses they had seen at the press conference, closely followed by an enormous truck carrying a bright yellow bulldozer and a small crane.

Then another truck, carrying two more bulldozers.

Then a third, loaded with a gigantic metallic object that was the shape of a truck-size shipping container, but had a door in its middle with two small windows on either side. There was already a label fixed over the door.

"This is *terrible!*" Allie said. She peered. "It says 'Site Office.'"

"Hah!" said Granda sourly, and for extra comment he made a loud sizzling sound by dropping several strips of bacon into a frying pan. This was rapidly drowned out by shouts and clangs from outside, as a gaggle of workmen emerged from the Trout bus and began unloading the trucks. To the back of the first truck they attached a long ramp, and drove the crane cautiously down it, heading for the truck with the container-office. The bulldozers chugged down an unloading ramp too, and trundled off in the direction of the next-door farm.

Granda, Tom and the twins ate bacon and eggs in a gloomy silence, until Allie could no longer bear it. She pushed a piece of bread fiercely into the toaster.

"What are they *doing*?" she said.

Jay got up, and went through the door connecting kitchen and store, peering out at the loch and the parking lot. "They're unloading that house-thing with the crane, on the far side of the lot."

"I don't mean right this minute, I mean what's it all about? How can they actually start building a hotel when the store is right in the way, and Granda won't sell?"

Her father said, "I think William Trout has declared war. He knows he can move fast, and he knows that the only things we can do to stop him will be very slow."

Outside the back door of the kitchen there was the muffled rattle of Portia leaning her bicycle against the wall, and she came in, hasty and upset.

"There are bulldozers out there!" she said. "Scooping up trees! Picking them up by the roots and dumping them in a pile! That beautiful old stretch of oak trees between the store and the old farm!"

Granda said, "In just a wee while they'll be digging up the farm, too."

"Stop them!" said Portia.

Tom sighed. "Just tell us how," he said.

"It's Sam Johnson's fault," Jay said. "Castle Keep's the only reason they came here. They're calling it the Trout Castle Resort, right? Why doesn't he just tell them they can't have the castle—that they can't even go near it?"

"Money," Granda said. He got up, and took his empty plate to the sink. "The Trout Corporation has bought him. Castle Keep doesnae mean hundreds of years of clan history to him and his brother, it means bills, bills, bills—to pay the rates, to patch the roof, to pay the guides. The money coming in from visitors covers maybe a quarter of that."

"He made it work until Trout came along," Allie said unhappily. Her piece of bread leaped out of the toaster, and she got up to rescue it. Beside her at the sink, Granda turned on the hot-water tap, and nothing came out.

They both stared.

Allie said, "Where's the water?"

She put down her toast and turned on the other tap. Nothing happened.

Portia said, "You have mains water, right, piped from Appin? You aren't on a well?"

"Aye, mains water," Granda said.

"It's those bulldozers!" Portia said. "They must have hit a pipe."

Granda said something very loud and angry in Gaelic, and dived for the door into the store. Everyone followed him, as he marched across the castle parking lot toward the Site Office, which the workmen had now installed on the opposite side from the jetty. Its door was open, and a young man in a Trout Corporation jacket was carrying in a box from one of the trucks.

"What are you people doing?" Granda demanded. "You've just cut off our water supply."

"Don't know anything about that," the man said. "We're just setting up. You'll want the Site Manager."

"Where is he?" said Portia.

"Not here yet. Like I said, we're just setting up. The office. And stuff for the new jetty."

"New jetty?" said Jay. "What's wrong with this one?"

"Too small," the young man said. He peered at them more closely. "You're those kids who were at the press conference, aren't you—well, you saw the model. A new jetty on the castle island, and a real big one here, so we can have a marina. People at the hotel and the condos, they'll all have boats."

He looked out at the road, where yet another truck was slowly approaching. "Ah," he said, sounding relieved. "Here's Freddy now."

This Trout Corporation truck was smaller than the others, but heavily loaded with bundles of planks and beams; it drew up beside the jetty. When Freddy climbed down, the twins saw that he was one of the chunky Americans who had interrupted their television interview the day before. He ambled toward them.

"You're the Site Manager?" Granda said. "I'm Angus Cameron. I live here. Someone's cut off the water supply to my house, I need it put back again. Now."

Freddy said, "I'll look into it." He waved to the workmen manning the crane, and they swung it over toward the load in his truck.

"*Now!*" said Granda.

"It goes right there," Freddy shouted to the workmen, and then he smiled politely at Granda. "Of course, sir," he said. "In the meantime, it would be safer for everybody if you'd all keep clear of our loading zone."

And he disappeared inside the door of the Site Office.

"*Listen!*" said the Boggart to Nessie. "*It's the invading man again! We have to help our people. They don't have an army to drive him out—what can we do?*"

The noise of trucks, bulldozers and crane had filtered into the library of Castle Keep, and woken them up. In the shape of seals, they were out in the loch, floating beside the jetty, staring across the parking lot in puzzled disapproval at the trucks, the crane, and the Site Office. The lumber from Freddy's truck was stacked on the shore, and the workmen had followed him into the office to make everyone a cup of tea.

In the store, Granda was waiting impatiently for his taps to start running again, and the twins were taking turns at watching whatever might happen next in the parking lot. Portia had gone off on her bicycle to see whether the bulldozers were still knocking down trees.

"Look at this," said Nessie to the Boggart. *"Here's how we can start."*

And he hauled his sturdy seal-body up on to the shore, nudged himself close to a bundle of planks, and pushed it into the water.

Then he gave a happy seal-honk, and did it again.

"Yes!" said the Boggart in delight, and he climbed out of the loch to do the same.

Watching from the store, Allie noticed the splashing, but could see nobody near it. She went outside to look more closely, and suddenly everyone heard her give a strangled shriek that was the sound of excitement trying to keep itself secret.

"Come quick!" she croaked. "It's the seals! Look what they're doing!" And Jay, Tom and Granda scrambled after her as she rushed toward the loch.

Two more piles of lumber splashed into the water. The Boggart and Nessie were lost in the pleasure of mischief, which has forever been the favorite occupation of boggarts. They hauled their ungainly seal-bodies back from the edge of the jetty toward the remaining stacks of lumber, paying no attention to Allie as she came skating up to them, with the others close at her heels.

Watching in disbelief, Allie started to laugh.

"Look at them! It's amazing! They're just seals, but it's as if they knew about old Trout!"

Jay said, grinning, "Granda, have you ever seen seals do that before?"

Granda was standing very still.

"I havenae," he said. "No indeed, I have never known a seal to behave like this."

He glanced over toward the Site Office, and then he looked at Tom.

There was something in the sound of his voice that made the twins look at their father too. He was staring at the seals, with an expression on his face that they had never seen before. The surprise and disbelief were there, but so was something else, indefinable, a kind of wonder.

Tom Cameron walked slowly toward one of the two seals. It was slightly smaller than the other, and as he approached, it pushed one more bundle of planks into the loch and splashed in after it.

Water sprayed over Tom's face and shirt, and he wiped it out of his eyes. But he was still gazing at the seal, and now he was beginning to smile.

He said, "Boggart?"

Allie blinked, puzzled.

The seal looked up from the water, out of its dark round eyes.

Tom said, "It's me, it's Tommy. I grew up. D'you remember me, Boggart?"

The head of the second seal emerged from the water, next to the first, and gazed at him.

"Nessie?" Tom said. "Is that you too, then? You stayed here, you never left!"

The two seals paused there, swaying with the small waves. They were both staring at Tom Cameron.

Tom said softly, in Gaelic, *"Tha mo chridhe maille ribh."*

The words seemed to hang in the air, like the echo of music. For a moment Allie felt almost as though time had stopped.

Then all at once the seals were gone. Neither Jay nor Allie saw them disappear under the water; they were just suddenly . . . not there.

Allie said, "What was it that you said?"

Her father seemed not to hear her.

Granda moved forward a little, and the two men stood together, father and son, the two faces echoing each other even though the hair above one was white and the other dark. They were both smiling, as though someone had just given them a wonderful present.

Jay and Allie stood watching them, bewildered.

Tom said, "He's back! *He's back!*"

Granda said, "I think you're right."

"And Nessie, too!"

"Both of them!" Granda said. "After all this time—it's been ten years or more."

"They're back!" said Tom again joyously.

Granda said, "I thought they'd just gone away, after you grew to be a man, an' left, and Mr. Mac died."

"They were sleeping. I bet they were sleeping. They can sleep for years and years, the old MacDevon said."

Jay said, "Who can sleep? What on earth are you guys talking about?"

His father paid him no attention whatsoever. Suddenly he gave a kind of happy yodeling shout, like an impulsive small boy, and he called out something else in Gaelic across the loch.

Allie said, baffled, "Is he calling the seals? Dad! What are you doing? What's *happening*?"

Granda put a comforting arm across her shoulders, but he was still smiling. He said, "Those two, they were not real seals, they had taken the shape of seals. It's hard tae tell the difference, but there is a trick of the light on the skin, if you have seen it before. They are shape-shifters, they can become anything they choose."

"They?" Jay said. *"Who's they?"*

Granda said, "Boggarts."

Allie looked up at him.

"Boggarts," she said.

"Very ancient creatures, of the Wild Magic," said their grandfather, whom they had never heard utter an irrational word before, in all their lives.

Jay said helplessly, *"Magic?"*

"The Wild Magic of the earth survives in the islands of Britain, and some other places," said their scientist father, smiling at them. "And its creatures have no beginning or end, they just *are*. There are very few of them left, and very, very few people are lucky enough ever to know them."

Jay and Allie stared at him.

And from the air over the rippling water of the loch, a voice came whispering to them in Gaelic, even though nobody was there.

SEVEN

Jay and Allie listened to the voice whispering across the water: a soft, hoarse voice that came out of nowhere.

They looked all round the loch. They looked at each other, and then at their father, as their world changed a little.

Tom Cameron smiled out at the invisible voice, and called out some more words in Gaelic. Then he raised a hand to the empty air over the loch, like a greeting, or a farewell.

Jay said, "This isn't really happening."

"But it is," Allie said.

"He said they're going back to the castle for a nap, because they're a wee bit tired," Tom Cameron said. He grinned. "And no wonder, after all that."

Jay said, trying hard to sound normal, "They live in the castle?"

"Well, they don't live anywhere in particular," said his father cheerfully. "But the Boggart's been around Castle Keep for centuries. The MacDevon clan were his people—and so we are too. He has a favorite place in the library where he likes to sleep—and Nessie, too, I guess. Oh, and he said they hoped you would sing the prince's song again—what does *that* mean, eh?"

Jay sat down abruptly on one of the remaining piles of lumber. "Uh," he said.

"When we went to the Seal Rocks with Portia," Allie said. "You sang for her. And there was a seal that looked at you, only you didn't notice. Oh my goodness."

Jay looked at Granda in helpless appeal. He said, "There are seals sleeping in the castle library and nobody's noticed?"

"Oh, they're only seals when they feel like it—they're invisible," Granda said. "I told you, they're shape-shifters, they can be anything or nothing. Nessie got his name because he spent a heck of a long time pretending to be the Loch Ness Monster."

"And nearly got stuck forever, and had to be rescued," said Tom.

Allie said slowly, "After Granda took his picture?"

"It's a long story," Granda said.

Jay said, "When Mom and Uncle Jess were kids, when Grandpa Robert inherited Castle Keep and they all came over— did they know about the Boggart?"

"Did they ever!" Tom Cameron said, laughing. "He lived with them in Toronto for three weeks—got taken there by accident in a piece of furniture. It was a triumph when we got him back again."

Jay and Allie stared at him, baffled.

Allie said, "Why didn't anyone ever tell us? Not even when we were here?"

Their father said, "Would you have believed it, before you heard the Boggart's voice?"

There was a long pause. Allie and Jay looked at each other.

"Well . . . no," Jay said.

There was a shout from the other side of the parking lot, and they saw that the American called Freddy had emerged from the Site Office with two of the Trout workmen. He came striding across to the jetty, staring at the water now puddling its surface, and then peered over the edge at the piles of wood submerged in the loch.

"What the—?" he said, and he stared at the twins, at Granda's white hair, and finally, disbelievingly, at Tom.

"You did this?" he demanded.

Jay said, "It was the seals."

"Oh sure," said the nearest workman. "You trained them, right?"

Freddy said slowly, "Maybe it was. That wood's real heavy. These folks couldn't move it."

"Six bundles—seven!" said the workman, leaning out over the water. "Crazy damn animals—we need someone on shotgun duty."

Granda said, "Seals are protected in Scotland, my friend. Bring a gun out here and your Mr. Trout will be in big trouble."

"Mr. Trout's going to bring big trouble for anyone interfering with this development," Freddy said. He unhooked a two-way radio from his belt. "I suggest you people do what I asked, and keep away from our loading zone. Whoever pushed this wood into the water, we're going to fish it out and nobody, *nobody* had better touch any construction material again."

Granda said, "This jetty may be your loading zone, but it's also where we keep my boat, for castle maintenance every week."

Freddy glanced at him without real interest, busy with his radio. "You won't be doing that anymore, didn't they tell you?" he said. "We do it from now on—part of the Trout agreement. Access to the castle is limited to Trout Corporation staff until the resort's up and running. And the castle's own jetty is terrible—we're building a new one. Top priority."

Granda's face froze into a very rare expression that the twins knew was a cover for rage. He said coldly, "And your top priority is putting back my water supply, which your construction has illegally cut off."

"I'll look into that," Freddy said.

"The Boggart and Nessie," Portia said, to the twins' astonishment. "Yes, Angus told me all about them. Lovely. My grannie was Welsh. She used to talk about a creature like that called a *pwca*. How wonderful if they're back."

She smiled compassionately at Allie and Jay. "I know it's hard to believe. Maybe Angus should show you Mr. Mac's letter."

They were all back in the store, and she had reported that the bulldozers and a team of workmen had begun to demolish the farmhouse next door. Out around the jetty, more workmen were splashing and shouting, trying to use the crane to rescue the piles of planks now lying at the bottom of the loch.

"No letter till I've reached the spineless Sam Johnson," Granda said, dropping the house phone back into its holder. He had already made three unanswered calls, and left three increasingly angry messages.

Portia said to Jay, "Just think of the boggarts as characters in a video game, only real."

"What was Mr. Mac's letter?" Allie said.

Tom said, "Where is it, Dad?"

"Bottom drawer of my desk, left-hand side," Granda said, and started pressing buttons again. By the time he had put the phone down once more, muttering, Tom was back with a leather folder in his hand. He put it down on the kitchen table, and the twins came peering as he opened it.

They saw a single sheet of paper with a crest at the top, and a handwritten letter set out neatly below. The handwriting was looped and graceful; it looked old.

Their father said, "You know about Mr. Mac, right? He was Sam Johnson's uncle."

"Yes, of course," Allie said. "The lawyer. Who bought Castle Keep from Grandpa Robert, who'd inherited it and never should have sold it."

"Hmmph," said Tom Cameron, though he didn't argue. "Well, when Mr. Mac moved into the castle, the Boggart started playing tricks on him—stealing things, stuff like that. Mr. Mac didn't know anything about boggarts, and he thought he was going mad. So even though he was a very levelheaded lawyer, he went up the stairs to the castle library and he took out a book he'd noticed called—what was it, Dad?"

Granda said, "*Hauntings of the Scottish Highlands and Islands.* It's still up there. And inside the book, to his great surprise, Mr. Mac found an envelope addressed 'To the New Owner of Castle Keep.' With a letter in it, written by Devon MacDevon, the last chieftain of the MacDevon clan."

"A lovely old man," Tom said softly.

"And this is what it said."

Granda picked up the folder, put a gentle finger on the letter, and began to read.

> *"So you've found him. And you have an intelligent head on your shoulders if you've come to this room and this book to find out what to do. I'd have liked to meet you.*
>
> *"Don't be feared of him. He means no harm, but his tricks will drive you wild if you let them. Be patient. He's older than you or me or the castle or the clan, and he'll be here when we're all gone. He's a thieving rascal, but he eats seldom and little. He likes porridge and cream and new wholemeal bread, apples and cheese, ice cream, ketchup, pickled onions and fish. Fish above all—he is kin to the seals, as are we MacDevons. And like us too, he enjoys his dram. But if you're short of whisky, he has a great taste for Ovaltine."*

Granda looked up at them. "Mr. Mac told me that he liked Ovaltine himself, and he had a full mug of it with him in the library when he was reading this. And he looked down at the mug and saw that it was empty."

"Wow," Jay said.

Granda read,

> *"He's a good soul, but he'll forget me when I'm gone. There's not but a few left like him, cousins here and there, not many. Have him stay, if you can. He's the Boggart of Castle Keep, and I'm fond of him. Good luck to you."*

He looked up again. "And then there was a line in the Gaelic. *'Tha mo chridhe maille ruibh.'*"

Allie tried to repeat it after him. "That sounds like what Dad said at first to . . . to the Boggart. At the loch."

"That's right," Tom said. "Well done. It means, *my heart is with you.*"

Outside, there was a great crash from the direction of the loch, and they saw that a load of rescued planks had slipped from the Trout Corporation crane. Half of them had splashed back into the water; the rest lay on the ground and the jetty, dripping.

"And all of this," Granda said, "is one more reason why hell will freeze over before I let Castle Keep become part of a Trout tourist development."

"They've already started," Portia said. "You should see what the old Robertson farm looks like now. How can you stop them?"

Tom Cameron said, "Maybe now we'll have a little help."

Freddy the Site Manager came stumping into the castle kitchen, puffing a little from his climb up the steps from the rocky shore, and dropped his rucksack on the floor. He flopped into a chair and put his feet on the table. It had been a long day, thanks to the need to pull all those drowned piles of lumber out of the loch. He wished he were in some comfortable local hotel, able to order himself a beer, preferably American and ice-cold and in a can. But William Trout had ordained that he should spend his first few nights in charge of Castle Keep, where nobody had lived for years and where the refrigerator was almost certainly empty.

He got to his feet, and checked. The refrigerator held two

bottles of water and a package of baking soda. Freddy sighed. Then he shivered suddenly. Within its thick stone walls, the castle was chilly, and growing dark. It was also unnervingly silent. He switched on the lights, took his cell phone out of his pocket and began playing some rock music for company. It sounded terrible, but it was comforting.

He was hungry, but there was nothing to eat except a sandwich and an apple in his rucksack, left over from lunchtime. He should have been able to buy food at the store run by old man Cameron, but for some reason it had closed early. What a pain that man was, turning down all the money he'd been offered to buy him out. Freddy had worked on three other William Trout developments before this, two in America and one in Ireland, but none of them had produced anyone as irritating and obdurate as Angus Cameron.

Freddy unwrapped his sandwich and turned up the volume of his music. It was a ham sandwich with more lettuce than ham inside it, and he was still hungry when he had eaten it. The apple didn't help much. Investigating the jars on the kitchen shelf, he found that one of them was full of tea bags; at least he could make himself a cup of tea. He found a kettle, took it to the sink and turned on the tap.

The tap made a small rattling sound, and no water came out of it.

Freddy said several words that he would not have said in front of his small son at home in New Jersey, and dropped the kettle into the sink. He remembered Angus Cameron's bitter complaints about the water supply cut off by the Trout bulldozers—which he had deliberately ignored, to teach

Cameron a lesson—and he realized, too late, that Castle Keep must rely on that same water supply. His own bulldozer had deprived him of his tea.

Now he had the two bottles of water in the refrigerator to last him until next morning, and he could choose between using them to make tea, or to wash his hands and face and clean his teeth. There was always the brackish water of the loch, but he didn't fancy the thought of clambering down the rocky steps with a bucket in the darkness.

Freddy sighed, and wished William Trout had never set eyes on the coast of Scotland. He took the two bottles of water out of the refrigerator, put them in his rucksack and went upstairs to find himself a bedroom. With him he took not only the rucksack but the music-blasting cell phone, to keep him company in the silent corridors—which, though he would never have admitted it, he found decidedly spooky.

First he found a bathroom, and used it, promising himself that he would flush its toilet with water from the loch in the morning. It occurred to him that Angus Cameron, with four people in his house, would be facing the same problem, but he felt satisfaction rather than sympathy.

Then he chose a bedroom, and found that underneath the tartan bedspread there were no sheets, but only some venerable and hairy blankets. Freddy said a few more cross words, and drank one of his bottles of water to cheer himself up. Then he attached his cell phone to its charger cord, stripped down to his shorts, wrapped himself in a hairy blanket, and lay down to rest.

Since he was alone in the castle, he saw no reason to turn his music off.

* * *

In the library, curled snugly beside Nessie in the gap between stones on a high shelf, the Boggart was jolted out of sleep by an intrusive sound he had never heard in the castle before: a rhythmic thumping sound, overlaid with a strange whining and the occasional loud shriek.

Suddenly he was wide awake, and resentful. He could feel Nessie stirring too.

"Did your people come over?" Nessie said, yawning. *"That's a terrible yawky noise out there. Is it supposed to be a singing?"*

The Boggart said crossly, *"It's the invading man again, or one of his fellows. Always breaking the peace. My people never behave so."*

He floated out into Freddy's bedroom, with Nessie following, and put a silencing finger on the cell phone. Freddy was now snoring, and did not stir. The Boggart looked round for some means of retribution. He found Freddy's sneakers, and tied their laces together. Nessie found his shirt and tied the sleeves in a knot; then took his pants, and tied the legs together in a neat bow. They looked in Freddy's rucksack and shared the water from his remaining bottle, which they left, empty, on his bedside table.

Then, in unspoken agreement, they wafted out into the night to check what Freddy and his workmen might have done while they had been taking their nap, and they were not pleased to see the piles of lumber back on the jetty—very wet, but lashed down this time with ropes in defense against marauding seals.

A night wind was blowing over the loch, sending small clouds scudding over the dark sky. The boggarts flew inland across the jetty, across the shore, over shadowy fields, and drifted past the rambling old farmhouse that had been there as long as they could remember, and its sheltering wood of oak trees. Through the dark wood they heard the scuffle of rabbits and hedgehogs and mice, and the grunt of a passing badger; they laughed as bats darted through them from tree to tree. A barn owl screeched softly, and the Boggart screeched back at her.

They flew higher, and at the edge of the wood they saw something they did not expect: trees lying uprooted, dragged out of the earth, left in rough heaps. They hovered there, making small sounds of sympathy and distress.

A half-moon rode in and out of the clouds above them, its light glimmering on the water, on the roof of Granda's store, and on something else, half-hidden beside the wood. Something yellow, gleaming.

The Boggart and Nessie flittered down toward it, and found themselves looking down at one of the bulldozers. They had seen many cars and trucks and buses in their time, but never a bulldozer.

"It's a machine."

"It's a nasty machine. Look, it's been digging up the trees!"

"It's sleeping now," Nessie said.

The Boggart said, *"It is."*

They looked at each other, and they flittered down through the darkness, down to their dying friends the trees, down toward the enemy.

EIGHT

Sam Johnson had finally called Granda back, full of apologies. He had said he would do his best to have the water supply restored, though he did point out gently that he had no responsibility for William Trout's development and his bulldozers.

"If you werenae selling him Castle Keep, his development wouldnae be here at all," Granda said bitterly.

"Ah well," said Sam Johnson. "Let's think of it as sharing the castle with more people."

Granda snorted. "Sharing! But not with the folk who've been looking after it for you all these years. We're banned frae going there now, you know that? Only Trout Corporation workers allowed in, until he's finished whatever monstrosity he's got in mind."

Sam Johnson said feebly, "Oh dear. But he has the right, doesn't he, if he's buying it. I'm sure it won't become a monstrosity. Oh dear. I thought he'd be using you and Portia, same as always."

"What else does he have the right to do?" demanded Granda. "Knock it down? Turn it into a casino?"

"I'm sorry, Angus. It's Eric—he's dying to sell to Trout, and wriggle out of the trust. I'd have been happy to buy him out and keep the castle—I even thought I might live there, when I retire. But there's no way I can match what Trout's offering."

"Your brother thinks only of money," Granda said. "He's as bad as Trout."

"I'm really sorry, Angus!" Sam Johnson said. He gave a long, unhappy sigh. "I'll talk to Eric again, I'll see if I can change his mind."

"Good luck wi' that," Granda said, and he had put down the phone.

And now he lay sleeping, dreaming of boggarts, dreaming his favorite dream of flying; dreaming of flying over a loch, its small waves crawling far below him, with a boggart flying on either side of him, holding his hand. Dreaming of a world with no William Trout and no threats of sewage overload, howling jet-skis, or roaring roads, but only green fields and grazing sheep, and taps that gushed fresh clean water when you turned them on.

Tom Cameron was dreaming too, dreaming of a day long ago when he was the age that his twins were now, when he had ferried the old MacDevon across from his castle to his parents' store in his little boat, as he did every week. When, inside the store, he had seen an apple rise up into the air with no visible support, because the Boggart had come shopping too. . . .

Allie was dreaming of the round dark eyes of a seal, a seal with a faint glow to its skin: a boggart seal who heaved himself around and dropped down toward the water of the loch, and then suddenly was not there at all. . . .

Jay, to his surprise even in sleep, was dreaming of driving a bulldozer.

Seated in his small inflatable Trout dinghy next morning, Freddy puttered over from Castle Keep to the shore in a very bad mood. He had gone searching through all the castle corridors and rooms, even up the stairs to the turrets; nobody was there. And nobody, for heaven's sake, would have come to the castle in the middle of the night to play a silly trick, and then gone quietly away again.

It was possible, perhaps, that he himself had woken up in the middle of the night feeling very thirsty, had drunk his bottle of water, and gone back to sleep and forgotten it. That could be why this bottle whose water he really, really needed was sitting here empty. But could he possibly have woken up and tied his shirt and pants and shoelaces into knots, and forgotten *that*?

Two Trout Corporation workmen were waiting for him on the decrepit little jetty; they took the bow line of his dinghy as it bounced on its own wake, and helped him out.

"Got something to show you," said one.

"Whatever it is, it can wait till I've had a cup of coffee," Freddy said grumpily, and he headed for his Site Office. He called back over his shoulder to the taller of the two men, "Joe! Just keep on clearing those trees."

"Can't!" Joe called back. "The bulldozer's in the loch!"

Freddy stopped. *"What?"*

They took him past Granda's store and along the shore, to the pile of uprooted trees that one of the bulldozers had made. Freddy had last been there the evening before, on his routine check of the day's work. Then, one bulldozer had been parked up at the old farmhouse that it was starting to demolish. The other had been sitting higher up, beside the pitted land where trees had been ripped out, waiting to start again the following morning.

But it wasn't there now, that second bulldozer; it was down in the loch, under the water. Only the yellow roof of its driver's cab poked up above the surface.

"Holy cow!" Freddy said. "Must have slid down the hill. Some fool parked it in neutral."

"I parked it," Joe said. "It wasn't in neutral, and the brake was full on. And the bucket was down."

"Are you sure?"

"Of course I'm sure," Joe said irritably. They were both big men, but he was several inches taller than Freddy. He was also Scottish, and although he was working for the Trout Corporation, he wasn't about to be doubted by an American.

"Okay, okay," Freddy said at once. "Then it's vandalism. I'll call the cops."

He thought about his knotted shirtsleeves. Then he thought about Angus Cameron's two grandchildren, and their hostile shouts at the press conference. He thought about Angus Cameron. He turned and looked along the shore toward the store.

"Get the other dozer," he said. "See if it can pull this one out. I'll be back in a few minutes."

* * *

The twins were looking out at a beautiful sunlit morning. Far out over Loch Linnhe, traces of mist still hung over the water, but the air in the kitchen was warm, and the windows were open. From the loch they could hear the high repeated call of a herring gull. Inside, there were only muted sounds from behind the door into the store, where Portia was on duty.

Allie said, "But if the Boggart and Nessie are going to help us, and they're in the castle and we can't go there, how do we get in touch with them?"

"We send them a message," Granda said, from the stove. It was breakfast time, and he was stirring a pan of porridge.

"How?"

Tom Cameron grinned. "Your granda is doing that right now," he said. "Boggarts can smell something they like to eat from a mile away. They don't actually need to eat, but if there's something around that they really fancy—remember the MacDevon's letter?"

"Porridge and cream," Jay said.

"And cheese, and pickled onions," said Allie. "What are pickled onions?"

"Little white onions, in vinegar."

"Eeeuw."

Granda tasted the porridge. "This is ready, so we don't need pickled onions. Give them their own dishes, d'ye think, Tom?"

"I think so. They prefer pinching things off your plate, but porridge is messier than a piece of bacon."

So four plates of porridge were set out on the kitchen table, with two empty plates at the end closest to the open window, waiting for boggarts.

"Cream!" said Jay, and fetched the jug from the refrigerator, to join the bowl of brown sugar. They all helped themselves, and there were some moments of contented silence, until Portia put her head round the door from the store.

"Want some porridge, Portia?"

"No thanks, I had breakfast. Angus, one of your favorite people is here to see you."

Granda looked at her expressionless face. "I take it you are speaking ironically," he said.

"You bet," said Portia.

"Can't you tell him I'm eating my breakfast?"

"He says it's urgent."

Granda sighed, put a plate over his porridge dish and went out with her into the store. There at the counter stood William Trout's unhelpful Site Manager, chunky and muscular, in a very rumpled T-shirt and jeans.

Freddy looked at Granda without pleasure and nodded.

"I called the water company," he said. "They're coming to fix the pipe."

"Good," Granda said.

"I also called the police, in case anybody gets any more bright ideas."

Portia said, "What d'you mean?"

Freddy said, keeping a close eye on Granda, "Did you hear any noise out there during the night?"

"Not after you lot stopped making it. Why?"

"Somebody drove one of my bulldozers into the loch. Was it you?"

Granda tried not to smile. "Now that's a great notion," he said. "But I've not got the remotest idea how to drive a bulldozer."

Portia scowled at Freddy. "Making false accusations is not just rude, it's slanderous," she said.

"And there were other things," Freddy said darkly.

"Were there now," said Granda.

"There'd better not be any more."

Suddenly Granda lost his patience with all things Trout. "I don't think I know your name," he said.

"Fred Winter," said Freddy.

"Good-bye, Mr. Winter," said Granda, and he went back into the kitchen. Tom and the twins, who had been listening at the door, backed hastily out of his way.

Granda closed the door behind him, sat down at the table, removed the plate from his porridge dish, and picked up his spoon.

Tom Cameron said, "I have a thought about who moved that bulldozer, Dad."

"Aye," Granda said, "I do too, but first I want my breakfast."

"Uurgh!" said Jay suddenly.

It was a strangled, wordless gasp, and past his pointing finger they saw the saucepan sailing through the air from the stove toward the empty dishes at the end of the table. The ladle filled the dishes with porridge; the saucepan sailed back to the stove; the cream jug rose into the air and poured cream first onto one dish and then the other.

Then the sugar bowl came hovering, and its spoon sprinkled sugar over porridge and cream. Quite a lot of sugar.

Then both dishes rose into the air, and hovered.

The Camerons sat down wordlessly to finish their breakfast, and there was no telling whether any small, busy slurping sounds were coming from visible or invisible mouths. But in a while, they heard in the warm air a low, happy sound like the purring of a cat. Two cats.

Allie and Jay sat listening, bemused, and the two dishes returned to the table beside them, empty.

Granda put down his spoon. "All right, Boggart," he said. "Tell me now, have you been at your tricks with the man's bulldozer?"

Nessie said to the Boggart, in their silent speech, *"What's a bull dozer?"*

"Does he mean the nasty machine, you think?" The Boggart gave a little happy bounce. *"He does! They've seen what we did!"*

Jay said in awe, "Could they really move a bulldozer, without driving it?"

"You'll be amazed what they can do," his father said.

"Yes!" said the Boggart proudly; he bounced again, and the Camerons saw the air seem to flicker for a moment over the kitchen table.

And somewhere out of the quivering air, his husky voice said softly, "Machine. Nasty machine."

Granda smiled. He said something in Gaelic; the Boggart answered, and so did another, lighter voice. Tom Cameron joined in, and Allie and Jay fidgeted in frustration at not being able to understand anything anybody said. It grew worse when both men and both unbodied voices began to laugh.

Tom turned to them, still smiling. "I'm sorry, we should stick to English—they're just more comfortable with the Gaelic. It's amazing they're talking to us at all—they never used to, ever."

"So what did they *say*?" Allie said.

"They did put the bulldozer in the water. They were planning to do the same to the other one, but Granda told them it wouldn't help for long."

"What made you laugh?" Jay said enviously.

"Nessie said maybe they should put Mr. Trout in the water."

"But are they going to get serious and help us? We have to *do* something! He's going to ruin this whole wonderful place!"

"They were trying," Tom said.

Allie said slowly, "They can't stop him by things like that, can they, and nor can we. He's one of those people who do just what they want, all the time. The only hope is to make him change his mind."

Out of the air, above their heads, the husky voice of the Boggart said, "Change his mind."

And another voice, lighter, said slowly, "The wee girl is right."

Allie and Jay sat very still, listening.

"Maybe she is, Nessie," Granda said.

The Boggart said, slowly, carefully, finding his words, "We havenae got an army—this is not like the old battles. It's the invader himself that has to decide he wants to take his machines away, and leave our place alone."

Nessie's voice said, "If we scared him?"

"Now there's a thought," Tom Cameron said.

"If we scared him enough," said the Boggart, uncertainly; he had always had much more fun from playing tricks on people than inducing terror.

"I know how to scare people," Nessie said happily, remembering his centuries in Loch Ness.

From the loch, wafting through the window on the summer air, came a noise none of them was expecting: a loud mechanical hoot, shattering the peace of the morning. It came again, twice, like the honk of a gigantic intrusive bird.

Granda said, "What on earth—?"

They peered out at the loch, and on the water beyond Castle Keep and its small green island, between the mainland and the coast of the island of Lismore, they saw a huge boat. It was a motor yacht, almost as big as the island ferry that made its peaceful way past them twice a day; its high white bow was facing them like a pointing finger.

"I know how to scare people," Nessie said again.

And as the boat slowly turned, they saw its name written large and proud along its side: TROUT QUEEN.

NINE

"He's back," said Jay. "He said he would be. 'In my yacht, the *Trout Queen.*'"

"A large and vulgar vessel, like its owner," said Granda.

They watched, as the massive boat moved slowly into shallower water beyond the castle, and they heard rattling noises as its anchor was lowered.

Allie said, "How can it be a yacht when it doesn't have any sails?"

"Motor yachts were invented for rich people who don't know how to sail," said Jay.

His father grinned. "Very true," he said. He turned away from the open window and spoke to the air above the two empty porridge plates.

"Boggart, have you seen this boat before?"

Then he said it again, in Gaelic.

There was a long silence. Granda and the twins turned too, wondering.

"Boggart?" Tom said. "Nessie? Are you still there?"

But there was no answer.

* * *

In their invisible, insubstantial boggart form, the Boggart and Nessie slipped through the water of the loch, pausing now and then to tickle a startled fish. Above their heads they heard a small buzzing sound, and they soared upward and saw Freddy the Site Manager bouncing across the small waves in his little inflatable dinghy, headed, as were they, for the *Trout Queen.*

"He's off to see the invading man," Nessie said. *"On the man's big boat."*

The Boggart said, *"The man has to go!"* He twirled in the water like a corkscrew, as if he might find an idea among the fish.

"I'm going to scare him away," Nessie said. *"I know how!"*

The Boggart stopped twirling. He said, *"You mean by turning monster?"*

"It scares them!" Nessie said happily. *"They scream!"*

"Oh, do take care," the Boggart said, worried. *"Ye munnae get stuck."*

Nessie laughed. *"Watch me!"* he said.

He began to glow very faintly, as boggarts do when they are thinking hard, and suddenly, there under the choppy surface of the loch, he took on the prehistoric shape in which he had once lived for hundreds of years, and he became the Loch Ness Monster. From his massive body a long, long neck rose, topped by a small head; he had flipperlike legs and a long, long tail. He was truly prehistoric.

He shot joyously round the Boggart in a circle, his enormous frame driven by great sweeps of the powerful tail.

"Look, cuz!" he cried. *"I'm back!"*

"Be careful!" the Boggart called, agitated. *"Be careful, cuz! Be*

sure you dinnae get stuck again, be sure you can change back!"

But Nessie was on his way, swimming fast toward the Trout yacht and diving down to the bottom of the loch. He found the boat's anchor, wedged only loosely into the mud, and he pushed his doglike head underneath it and closed his jaws round the anchor chain. Then he shot up toward the surface, with the Boggart in nervous pursuit.

Freddy's empty dinghy was bobbing beside the yacht, and Freddy was up on the high foredeck, with two other men and the tall, bald, imposing figure of William Trout.

In a great spray of water, Nessie broke the surface, his long grey-green neck towering over the boat, and he dropped the anchor on the deck, amidships. He opened his mouth, showing rows of alarmingly pointed long teeth, and gave a shattering bellow like the grunting roar of an angry hippopotamus.

Freddy and the two sailors cowered away, crouching to escape the teeth. Nessie dripped mud and water all over them, and they found themselves breathing air that reeked of fish and seaweed, like the low-tide stink of a muddy beach.

Cries of alarm came from other parts of the boat, and its engine started up again.

Snarling, Nessie peeked down at William Trout, waiting happily for his shriek of terror.

But William Trout wasn't scared. He gazed at Nessie in astonishment and disbelief, and slowly the astonishment changed to delight. "It's the Loch Ness Monster!" he cried. "Look! Just like the picture! It has to be! We've got the Loch Ness Monster in our loch here!"

He beamed up at Nessie, a broad white smile on his

suntanned face, and he went on beaming even as Nessie raised his head and roared again.

"This is wonderful!" he cried. "The whole world will come! Terrific, just terrific!"

He reached into his pocket, pulled out his cell phone and began frantically shooting a video of Nessie. "Freddy!" he yelled. "Get up, man—get pictures, quick!"

The Boggart whirled round Nessie's enormous tail and shot up out of the water, invisible but highly agitated. "*Dive, cuz! Dive! It's no' working!*"

Nessie gave a final angry roar, sending a blast of warm fishy air at William Trout, and dropped back into the loch.

Mr. Trout, flushed with excitement and triumph, gazed longingly down at the swirling water, and then all around, in the hope that the monster would reappear. He shook his head at Freddy and the sailors, getting to their feet and shaking off water and scraps of weed.

"Chickens!" he cried. "Chickens, all of you! Good thing one of us has his head screwed on! This is amazing! Fantastic! You realize what a tourist draw this will be for us? Just wait till I tweet about it! *Look, folks, this is why there hasn't been a clear sighting of the Loch Ness Monster in Loch Ness in twenty years— he's mine now! I've got him!*"

He spun round, clutching his phone, staring out at the water, but there was still no sign of movement. A few strands of seaweed bobbed up and down in the small waves.

The *Trout Queen*'s engine gave a throaty snarl, and the boat began to move away from the castle, farther up the loch. Two more crewmen came hurrying forward and grabbed the anchor and its chains, carrying them to the bow, and after them came the boat's captain, scowling, heading for William Trout. He was a stocky, grey-haired Scot named David Macdonald; he had come with the yacht when Trout bought it from its previous owner the year before, and he was not happy at the change.

"I told you she'd drag her anchor," he said crossly. "It's the wrong place—the bottom won't hold."

William Trout's voice rose in disbelief. "You didn't *see*?"

"See what?" said David Macdonald.

"The Monster, man! The Loch Ness Monster! Right here, leaning over us—can't you smell the stink it made? And our anchor didn't drag—the Monster pulled it up!"

"Tell me another one," David Macdonald said.

"It's true," Freddy said. "Look at the mess it made!"

Still dripping, he waved his arms over the pools of water and seaweed on the deck.

"The mess *you* made," said David Macdonald. "Been swimming, eh, Freddy?"

William Trout was busy with his cell phone. "Look at this, then!"

David Macdonald sighed. "The Loch Ness Monster is a fabrication," he said, "kept alive only by the imaginations of gullible tourists."

"Here you are!" said Mr. Trout triumphantly. "Just you wait! Look at this!" And he pressed the small play arrow on his screen.

They all looked, and saw a short, uneventful video of Castle Keep and the loch, with the railing of the *Trout Queen* in the foreground.

"Very nice," said David Macdonald.

Mr. Trout cursed loudly, and his fingers talked to his phone. Obediently it showed him, over and over, the landscape at which its camera had been pointed—but with no sign of Nessie in the picture at all.

David Macdonald rolled his eyes, and headed for the wheelhouse. "Excuse me," he said. "I have work to do."

"Where's it gone?" shouted William Trout in fury. "I had its picture, clear as day—where's it gone?"

Nessie headed for the deep water, great sweeps of his powerful tail driving him south, away from the *Trout Queen* and Castle Keep. His head was just above the water, his long neck thrust out straight; his legs steered him like the flippers of a seal. The Boggart, invisible, whizzed along in pursuit.

"That's enough, cuz! Change back!"

"But it's fun!" Nessie called. *"I'd forgotten the feel of it! It always was fun!"*

"Change back! You're a boggart! The Monster shape was to scare the man, and the man wasnae scared!"

Nessie slowed down. He sighed.

"You'll get stuck!" the Boggart yelled.

"Oh, all right," Nessie said regretfully, and in an instant his massive body was gone, and he was a boggart again: weightless, formless, invisible, an embodiment only of energy and enchantment and mind.

He turned a somersault around the Boggart. *"That's an unnatural man,"* he said. *"I did my best. I scared all of them but him. And he laughed! He was pleased!"*

The Boggart said unhappily, *"He made pictures of you with his little camera-thing."*

"No," Nessie said. *"I saw to that. No more pictures, not since I left my loch, not ever. They can see me, but their camera-things can't."*

He turned another somersault, and a small school of pollock swam through him and scattered in alarm. Then he slowed down again, sobered by a thought. *"But he wasnae scared,"* he said. *"How do we scare him away?"*

The Boggart thought hard, and began to glow a little. Though boggarts have very little care for memory over the centuries of their long, long lives, he tried to look back through the years to a distant time that might give him an idea. For an instant, flickering in the depths of his mind, he saw the image of a horse.

Then it was gone.

"The Old Things," he said. *"Our people have no clan left, and no army, so we must get help from the other Old Things."*

Nessie drifted through the water in silence for a moment. *"It's been so long,"* he said. *"Are they still here?"*

"If we're here, they are too," the Boggart said. *"We'll find them. And one of them will help us fight the invading man."*

He smiled to himself, a small, ominous smile.

"Maybe he has to meet the Each-Uisge," he said.

From the store, it had been the twins who first saw the long prehistoric neck rise out of the water, as they gazed disdainfully across the loch at the *Trout Queen*.

"Dad! Is that Nessie?"

"Granda! It's just like your photograph!"

"Oh my Lord," Tom Cameron said. "That's our Nessie all right, back in monster mode. That's where they went!"

"To scare away William Trout," Granda said. "But will it work?"

And Allie had grabbed her cell phone and taken pictures, over and over again, for as long as the huge prehistoric body was towering there over the boat. Nessie was a long way out on the loch and rather blurry, but he filled the frame, and Allie gazed at the little screen, fascinated.

But when he had dropped back into the water, and everyone gathered round as Allie played back the photographs and video captured on her phone, there had not been a sign of Nessie in any of them.

"I guess he didn't want his picture taken," said Tom to his disappointed daughter. "The only thing he wanted to do was scare the daylights out of Trout."

"He let Granda take his picture," said Allie sadly.

"That was in Loch Ness," Granda said. "And he wants everyone else in the world to think he's still there."

Before long they heard the door of the store crash violently open, and at once William Trout's big voice was filling the air, calling, insistent.

"Angus Cameron! I need to talk to Angus Cameron!"

Portia's voice said calmly, "He's not available."

"Well, make him available," said William Trout. "Tell him it's me."

"That will have no effect at all," Portia said.

Granda sighed. "She's a great watchdog," he said, "but she'll not be a match for this one. An attack dog, that's him.

And from the sound of him, Nessie's only managed to make him worse."

He went out into the store, where William Trout's gleaming bald head was brushing against the helium balloons that bobbed along the ceiling, for sale to the smallest tourists. Everyone followed him.

"Mr. Trout?" said Granda.

Trout glared at him, exasperation now mixed with a kind of respect. "You knew, didn't you? The Loch Ness Monster, here in Loch Linnhe! *That's* why you want to keep me out! You knew the Monster was here, you knew what a huge success that would be for the resort. Well, you can't stop me now—I've seen him! I'll tweet it to the world!"

"Will you now?" said Granda. "And will the world believe you?"

"Are you joking?" said Mr. Trout with scorn. "When it comes from the Trout? Besides, I have witnesses."

"But do you have proof?" Granda said.

"Of course," Mr. Trout said, and his cold blue eyes stared at Granda, and Granda knew that he was lying.

He said, "The Loch Ness Monster belongs to Loch Ness, Mr. Trout. Would you like a copy of the photograph I took there?"

"Twenty-five pounds," Portia said helpfully, pointing to the array of framed photographs high on the wall. "Or thirty euros."

"I have one already," William Trout said. In spite of his hostility, his voice filled with happy triumph. "And never mind old photographs! However it happened, we have the real Monster, here, now—and we're going to get a picture of him!

You *know* how that will excite people! *Everyone* will come to see it! The Trout Castle Resort will be world-famous! Maybe we can tame him!"

Tom Cameron said, "Maybe you should wait to announce the Monster until you have another sight of him, Mr. Trout."

William Trout glanced at him as if he were an annoying insect. He said loftily, "We've set up a twenty-four-hour watch. The next sighting will give us pictures that go round the globe."

Then he turned back to Granda, and making a determined effort, he gave him a big friendly smile. "Angus, I'm making you one final offer for this house and the store. Seven hundred and fifty. Three-quarters of a million pounds. Far more than it's worth, but I'm a generous man."

Allie and Jay looked at each other with wide eyes.

"No," Granda said.

Mr. Trout's smile vanished. "You'll regret it," he said. "Boy, will you regret it!"

Granda said, "I doubt that very much."

Outside, from the edge of the loch, there was a sudden loud roar followed by a gigantic splash, as the first bulldozer tried to pull the second out of the water, and failed.

TEN

The Boggart and Nessie whirled away from the *Trout Queen*, past the Seal Rocks and Castle Keep, down through the Lynn of Lorn, which is the water that divides Lismore Island from the coast of Argyll, and they paused beside the quiet island called Eilean Dubh, where nobody lives.

The Boggart was trying hard to remember. *"The Old Things,"* he said. *"The Old Things . . . it's been so long. . . ."*

Nessie said, *"There was an Old Thing came to my loch, before the English blew up my clan's castle. She was a wailer, she screamed us a warning . . . the Caointeach, that was her name."*

"Yes! Of course! She lived here, here in Argyll!"

"She lived by a waterfall."

"Yes! Oh, well done, cuz! Come!"

And the Boggart whirled them out of the water, over the loch, over the coast and the beginning of hills, to a river that crashed down over rocks in a waterfall, where once otters used to play. He remembered the otters. He thought he remembered the Old Thing called the Caointeach.

They hovered, invisible and motionless, on the rocky lower bank of the river, and the droplets of falling water filled the air around them and made a rainbow all across the falls.

"Caointeach!" called the Boggart. "Oh Caointeach! A greeting from an Old Thing to an Old Thing!"

Nessie called too. "A greeting, Caointeach!"

They watched and waited, waited and watched.

And very gradually, on the shining wet rocks at the foot of the waterfall, the Caointeach took shape. She was a very small old woman in a green gown, with a high-crowned white cap on her head.

She looked at them, and she scowled.

"What?" she said.

"A greeting!" said the Boggart.

"That's it?" said the Caointeach.

"Well, yes," the Boggart said, a little deflated.

"A very warm greeting!" said Nessie hopefully.

The Caointeach looked at them without enthusiasm, but she sat down on a rock, spreading her green skirt around her, and she put her bare feet into the water.

"That's something, at least," she said. "Nobody listens these days for the Caointeach. No clan cares for a warning. Half of them have never even heard of an Old Thing."

Nessie said, "Do you not scream out as you used to, before a disaster comes to a clan?"

"I could scream my head off," said the Caointeach bitterly, "and they'd not hear. They have little machines with screens in their hands, and things in their ears, and that's all they listen to and see. The clans are not what they were. And nor am I."

"Oh, you are so," the Boggart said. "You are wise, you know all the Old Things. So we come to you for advice, to help us get rid of one of the worst of the people with machines."

The Caointeach said, *"What has this person done?"*

"He is destroying the peace of our beautiful loch, he has cut down our trees, he would cover the green fields with brick and tar, he is building an enemy castle and threatening our own clan castle. He is terrible!"

Nessie said, *"We want him to go away, and so do our people."*

"Hum," said the Caointeach. *"He is a Changer."* She tucked a wisp of hair into the white cap on her head, which was the shape of a round-topped loaf of bread and had certainly not changed for at least two hundred years.

"Usually," she said, *"these Changers strip the land of everything but grass, and then cover it with people who spend all their days hitting a tiny white ball with a long thin stick."*

"He would do that too, I daresay," said the Boggart, *"but there is already a place like that not far away, which he can use."*

The Caointeach made a disapproving sound like a loud click. *"Your loch has problems enough,"* she said. *"This person should leave it alone. I shall summon up an Old Thing to drive him out. The question is, which one?"*

A hint of malice came back into the Boggart's eye. *"The Each-Uisge, perhaps?"* he said.

The Caointeach blinked. *"Are you sure?"*

"Yes!" the Boggart said.

"Very well," the Caointeach said, and she stood up on her rock, straightening her green skirt and checking her cap once more. She raised her head, curved her hands round her mouth, and called into the air some words in a language that even the boggarts did not understand.

They waited. Nothing happened.

The Caointeach made her clicking sound again, and

stamped her bare foot on the rock. She called out the same words, irritably, louder.

"Well?" said a voice, also irritable. "What is it, then?"

The voice came from the river below the waterfall, and they saw a young man there, standing barefoot at the edge of the water with his trousers rolled up to his knees. He was wearing a white shirt and a baseball cap and holding a fishing rod.

The Boggart thought: *This is the Each-Uisge? I didn't think he looked like that. And he isn't even speaking the Old Speech.*

Then he noticed that the young man was quite astonishingly handsome. He had rather long brown hair, curling over his neck, and bright blue eyes, and his face had perfect classical good looks in spite of its peevish expression.

"I'm busy," said the young man.

"Two Old Things need your help, Each-Uisge," said the Caointeach. "Shape-shifters, boggarts. They have an enemy."

The young man brightened a little, and put down his fishing rod. "Is the enemy a man or a woman?" he said.

"A man," said the Boggart, puzzled.

The young man smiled, a smile full of beautiful white teeth. "Ah well," he said, "in that case . . ."

And suddenly he was not there, and in his place was a horse: a gleaming brown Arab stallion, as handsome as the young man had been. It shifted restlessly, one hoof driving at the riverbank, and water splashed all around it, glittering.

"At your service," said the horse.

The Boggart felt his memory flicker, and he relaxed.

"Each-Uisge," he said, "there is a man named Trout who is attacking our loch, and we want him to go away."

"Not a problem," said the horse. "So long as he likes to ride."

"I'm sure he can ride a horse," said the Boggart. "He is the kind of man who wants to be good at everything."

"Excellent," said the horse. He pranced in a circle, splashing through the water. "In that case, all you need to do is lead me to him."

The Caointeach was sitting on her rock again, her green skirt spread around her like seaweed. "Excuse me," she said, "but I think we should also mention what happens after that."

"Easy," said the Boggart confidently. "Once he's sitting up on the Each-Uisge's back, he's stuck there, he can't move. So he just gets taken away."

"And he'll never want to come back," Nessie said. He beamed. "And our people will be so happy."

"There's just one little thing," the horse said.

"There is indeed," said the Caointeach.

"I don't just take him away," the horse said. "I eat him."

The Boggart and Nessie became very still, which is not a common state for a boggart unless he is asleep.

"You *eat* him?" the Boggart said.

The horse said proudly, "I am the Each-Uisge—my way is traditional. When a man is on my back, he cannot get off, and I dive into the loch and he drowns. And then I eat him."

He smiled, as if at a happy memory. "They're usually delicious," he said.

The Boggart and Nessie gazed at him in dismay.

"All except the liver," said the horse. "I've never fancied liver. So the man's liver floats up to the surface of the loch. I think of it as a present for the birds."

"Specially the herring gull," said the Caointeach. "He'll eat anything."

"Oh dear," the Boggart said. "I didn't remember the eating part."

Nessie said, "I really don't think our people want to kill the Trout person. They just want him to go away."

They hovered together in the spangled air above the waterfall, each feeling the other's unhappiness. Boggarts are mischief makers, boggarts love to cause trouble and play tricks, but boggarts do not take life. On the whole, they feel they were put into the world to make life more interesting.

"Tenderhearted, eh?" said the horse. "Well, suit yourselves. I'll go back to my fishing, then."

He shook himself, spraying them with glittering drops of water, and in an instant the horse was gone and the handsome young man was there again, standing half in and half out of the water, tying a fly onto the end of his fishing line. He looked up at them, and at the Caointeach.

"I plan to catch a trout," he said. "And I have to tell you, I shall eat it."

The Boggart looked from him to the Caointeach and back again. Though he had vague memories of the MacDevon clan of Castle Keep, who had certainly not been averse to destroying their enemies, he had trouble remembering much about his own kind, the Old Things.

"Is there not another Old Thing that could rid us of the Trout person without killing him?" he said. "Send him away full of fear?"

"The Baobhan Sith?" said the Caointeach to the Each-Uisge.

"W-el-l-l," said the young man. "Maybe the Spriggans. Or the Luidaeg of Skye."

Nessie said helpfully, "The Trout person is on a boat. It's big and noisy, just like him."

"Ah," said the young man, and he gave the Caointeach a beautiful smile.

"Of course," said the Caointeach.

They said together, "The Blue Men of the Minch."

The Boggart thought about this. He remembered the name, but that was all.

"The Minch is a long way from here," he said.

"Oh, not so far for a boggart," said the Caointeach.

"Can you not summon them for me?"

"Certainly not," said the Caointeach. "The Blue Men belong to the Western Isles, and their business is to defend their place. You'll not move them, you'll have to ask them for help, and then lure your man up there. But the Blue Men are what you need."

"They are," said the young man. "And I wish you well, boggarts. Now you have taken up enough of our time."

And he, and his fishing rod, disappeared.

The Caointeach was still sitting on her rock beneath the ghostly rainbow of spray, but she was beginning to fidget. One bare foot splashed restlessly up and down as the river rushed over it.

"Thank you, Caointeach," said the Boggart. "Thank you for your help. Is there anything we can do for you in return?"

The Caointeach thought for a moment, and a soft, wistful look came over her lined face. "Bacon," she said.

They stared at her.

Nessie said, "Are you serious?"

"Crisp, crunchy bacon," said the Caointeach dreamily. "I think of it often. It's been such a long time—a hundred years or so."

"We know just where to get that," said the Boggart, "but it may take a wee while."

"That's lovely," said the Caointeach. "Go to the Minch, and good fortune go with you. I've waited this long, it's no harm to wait some more."

She stood up, shaking the spray from her green skirt, and she smiled at them.

"Bacon," she said softly, happily to herself, and she too disappeared.

While the Boggart and Nessie had been gone, Granda had started an anti-Trout petition. It was a plea to the local council, asking that for environmental reasons, they should prevent William Trout from building his lavish Trout Castle Resort on the peaceful shore of Loch Linnhe. It quoted scientific studies of polluted lakes and vanished wildlife, it warned of peril to small aging roads and bridges, it showed proof that Trout resorts in other places had promised local jobs and then brought in their own employees instead. Granda and Tom had written it together, adding photographs; it was an impressive document.

Jay and Allie printed out many copies from Granda's computer, and rode bicycles to every store and library for miles around to try to convince people to hang one on their notice boards, to attract signatures. When they had run out of public buildings, they began knocking on people's doors.

"But he already has the council's permission," Allie said. "Some people tell us that and just shake their heads, like, why bother?"

"Those who give permission can take it back," Granda said.

"Or at least, we hope so," said Tom. "Look, here come some more castle gazers."

The twins reached for their petition clipboards, as a car drove up to join the seven already parked outside the store. The parking area between store and shore, from which visitors had always viewed Castle Keep in the past, was now largely enclosed by a tall, ugly wire fence and labeled CONSTRUCTION SITE: KEEP OUT. And the drowned bulldozer, finally rescued and restored, was lumbering to and fro with three others, as workmen in the jackets labeled TROUT began demolishing the next-door farm.

A mother, a father, a small boy and a very small girl descended from the car and gazed in dismay at the fence and the roaring bulldozers. Jay and Allie tumbled out of the store door to follow them, as they wandered about trying to find a clear view of Castle Keep. Tourists who arrived solely to see and photograph the castle were their favorite quarry.

The father looked round as they approached, and he waved at the fence. "What's all this, then?" he demanded. He sounded English, and he had a camera dangling from his neck.

"There's an American trying to build a big resort hotel," Jay said.

"What a shame," said the mother. "We were here two years ago and it was so lovely and peaceful."

"And did you see the seals then?" said Allie.

"Yes!"

"I saw a *big* seal," said the small boy. He had thick dark hair and wide serious eyes, and his toddler sister was clutching his hand.

Allie sighed. "They don't come anymore," she said sadly. This was not strictly true, since the seals were curious creatures and came to investigate the construction work from time to time, but Allie had decided that since Mr. Trout had no conscience, her own could take a few minutes' rest too.

Jay got down to business. With one hand he held out his clipboard to the disappointed parents; with the other he offered them a pen. "Everyone's signing a petition to stop the development from spoiling the loch," he said. "Would you like to sign it too?"

The father eyed the clipboard suspiciously. "I don't know about that," he said.

But the mother put out her hand at once. She read the petition carefully. "Oh come on, Chris," she said, "it's a good cause," and she took Jay's pen and wrote down her name and address.

"What's that for?" said the boy who had seen the seal.

"It tells people I want all this mess to go away," said his mother, and she handed the clipboard to her husband.

"Oh well," he said, and signed.

"Can I sign it too?" said the little boy.

They all looked at Jay.

"I don't see why not," Jay said. "Allie and I have."

The little boy handed his sister to his mother, took the clipboard from his father, sat down on the ground and wrote very carefully on the petition, PETER WILSON AGE 6. I LIKE SEELS.

"Thank you, Peter," Jay said.

The nearest bulldozer disappeared in the direction of the doomed farm, taking the roar of its engine with it, and suddenly in the unexpected quiet they heard a honking sound from the water beyond the jetty. A head rose from the surface of the loch, a whiskered head like the head of a dog, with large dark eyes. It gazed at them for a moment, and then it was gone.

Allie and Jay heard a husky voice in the air, close to their ears but so soft that perhaps nobody else could hear it.

"Twins!" it said. "Twins, listen!"

"It's the Boggart!" Jay whispered.

"A seal!" cried the little boy.

Allie said hastily, "You're so lucky, Peter! He came to say thank you to you! Thank you for signing!" And for his parents, she pointed to the end of the jetty. "If you go over there, you can still get a good shot of the castle," she said. "Maybe you'll get the seal, too, if he hasn't gone. Or you could walk to the Seal Rocks."

"And we're all allowed on the jetty," Jay said, "so don't let anyone tell you to get off it."

The father raised one hand to him, clutched his camera with the other, and marched off toward the jetty, with his family following.

Jay and Allie looked all around, at the loch, at the air, at the machine-littered land.

"Boggart?" Allie said softly. "Are you there?"

Round their heads, the air rippled a little, and the husky voice came again.

"Going for help," it said. "Going to the Minch. Following the invading man, to scare him away."

Gradually it grew more distant, so that they could hear it only for a few seconds,

"Going to the Minch . . ."

Then it faded away.

"What's the Minch?" said Jay.

Allie said, "Let's go and ask Dad."

ELEVEN

William Trout was standing beside his captain, David Macdonald, on the foredeck of the *Trout Queen*. He suspected the puffy clouds in the Highland sky of threatening rain, so he was wearing his waterproof Trout Corporation jacket, black with the letter *T* in bright yellow on the back. David Macdonald was the only member of the crew who declined to be seen in this jacket, and was wearing a sweater.

"Well," said Trout, "if you won't take me to Loch Ness, we'll go somewhere else. I don't need to go there anyway—I'm positive the Monster's right here."

David Macdonald sighed. "It's not that I won't take you, it's that the way to Loch Ness is complicated and this boat is too big. "

"Whatever," said Trout. "Plus the fact that you don't believe we saw the Monster."

"Your camera didn't see it," said David Macdonald.

William Trout said loftily, "There's no point in arguing, Macdonald. I know what I saw, and it's going to help the Trout Castle Resort make history. Freddy has guys with cameras watching in four different locations. We'll get him, we'll get him for sure! And for now I just need a little side trip. To a golf course, maybe. My wife's in London shopping for a few days, and I'm not about to sit here waiting for her."

He glanced over the side, and then looked more closely. "Is that a seal down there?"

In the choppy water below, a rounded head surfaced for a moment. Then another. They ducked below the surface, then reappeared. It was almost as though they were looking up at William Trout.

"Seals seem to like you," David Macdonald said. "Though I hear they had a try at tossing some of your building materials into the loch."

He looked at Trout with a grin, waiting for a reaction, but got none. William Trout was still staring down at the water, even though the seals had disappeared again. He seemed to be not just looking, but listening.

"The Hebrides," he said. "The Outer Hebrides. Let's go up there."

"You never mentioned that before."

"Well, now I have," William Trout said. "I just suddenly thought of it. It's an excellent idea." He sounded as certain as he always did, but this time there was a faint note of surprise in his voice as well. "And by the time we get back, they'll have a picture of the Monster."

"The Isle of Lewis is beautiful," David Macdonald said fondly. "And they have a golf course up there, in Stornoway. But we'll likely have some rough water getting there."

"Nothing I can't take," said William Trout, drawing himself up, tall and self-confident. The sun shone out between clouds and gleamed on his bald head.

"Very well then," said David Macdonald. "Off we go, to risk our way through the Minch."

"He's going," the Boggart said. *"I put the picture in his head."*

"Aye," said Nessie. *"Well done. A pity we can't get rid of him the same way."*

"Well," the Boggart said, *"we mun get there before him. Come on!"*

Dropping their seal shape, they rose out of the water and became formless, disembodied boggarts again. Off they went, keeping ahead of the *Trout Queen,* and they went a long way. Through Loch Linnhe they flittered, and up into the misty air and over the green hills and small lochs toward the Western Isles. Below them were the islands of the Inner Hebrides, Coll and Muck and Eigg and Rum and Canna, lying in the sea like sleeping animals, and they wandered past these and over the greater island of Skye, and so toward the Outer Hebrides.

It was a very long time since the Boggart had seen the Western Isles, and Nessie, born into an inland loch, had never seen them at all. But both of them knew they were at home. The Hebrides were part of the heritage of all the Old Things of Scotland, or perhaps it was the other way round and the Old Things were the heritage of the Scots, and of the Norsemen who had come to these islands a thousand years ago.

Now, dropping down past the island of Skye, they were over the fierce stretch of ocean called the Minch. Farther down they went, down through the dark salt water, down to the caves where the Blue Men live. Blue heads poked out of the caves as they passed, and long blue hands groped through the water—but found nothing, for a boggart is an Old Thing, and when he chooses to be invisible, not even another Old Thing can see him.

The Boggart called out, *"Where is the Chief of the Blue Men?"*

"Farther down, farther down," said thin voices from the caves.

So they swam farther, down and down.

"We have a message for the Chief of the Blue Men!" Nessie called.

"Farther down," hissed the voices. *"Farther down!"*

And at last, though they were nowhere near the bottom of the sea yet, they came to a cave that was a wide opening in one of the towering underwater columns whose peaks are the Shiant Islands, and they saw blue light shining out of it like a beacon: an arm of light, stretched out into the darkness.

"Who are you?" said a deep voice out of the blue glow. *"Who are you, to call the Chief of the Blue Men?"*

The Boggart was not used to being formal, but he tried to remember the right words with which to be polite to another Old Thing.

"I am the Boggart of Castle Keep," he said, *"and this is my cousin, the Boggart of Loch Ness. We bring greetings, and we beg assistance from the Blue Men of the Minch, to drive away a threat to the peace of our shores."*

"Well," said the deep voice, *"you know that our trade is in ships, and indeed we drive them away, we drive them to the bottom of the sea. Is your threat inside a ship?"*

"He is, at the moment," said the Boggart. *"There's just one thing—we don't want to drive him to the bottom of the sea, we only want to drive him away. Away from Scotland, away from our places and our people."*

"Human people?" said the voice.

"Well, yes," said the Boggart. *"Our friends."*

"And seals," Nessie said.

"Hmm," said the voice, and within the blue beam of light now they saw the face of the Chief of the Blue Men: an angular, commanding face with strands of blue hair waving around it, and its chin wreathed in the drifting locks of a long blue beard.

"Well," said the Chief, *"we have our tradition, and if your threat person obeys it, I am bound to set him free. If he does not, I promise you that his boat will go away and never come back again."*

He paused, and raised his head, looking up so that hair and beard flowed down in a blue parallel, and the Boggart and Nessie heard what he was hearing: the distant thrum of engines, high up on the surface of the sea. Without another word he dived out of his blue-lit glow and upward, and all around and above them the water seemed suddenly to boil, as blue figures came whirling out of the caves and rose in a great cloud, heading for the engine noise.

The Boggart and Nessie followed, keeping their distance.

"Is it the invader's boat?" Nessie whispered.

"I hope so," the Boggart said.

"What will happen?"

"Do you not know?"

Nessie twitched, as a large salmon dived through him to avoid a fleeting Blue Man. *"I come frae an inland loch, cuz. It's only from you I've learned the ways of the creatures of the sea."*

"Well, it's a contest," the Boggart said. *"I'm remembering, now. If you sail through the Minch and you cannae match the Blue Men in rhyming, they will sink your ship. Their leader calls out a verse, and*

it has to be answered in verse, and they wait, ready to pull you down. Look—take care!"

He dived sideways, since they had risen to the level of the *Trout Queen*, and above them they saw not the boat itself but an immense cluster of blue tails and bodies. It was the Blue Men, clinging to the sides and keel of the *Trout Queen*. They covered every inch of it except the stern, with its two enormous propellers, and the propellers thrashed vainly, unable to move the boat at more than a snail's pace while the weight of the Blue Men held it back.

Up on the deck, on the wildly rocking boat, William Trout was clutching the rail. He yelled at David Macdonald, "You didn't warn me the seas would be this dangerous up here!"

David Macdonald said nothing. He was fighting to hold the boat on course, baffled by the fact that although the engine was set for full ahead, they were hardly moving at all. And though he was a firmly rational man, with no patience for fanciful reports of the Loch Ness Monster, a small insistent voice at the back of his head was reminding him of the stories his grandmother had once told him of the Blue Men of the Minch. He was trying very hard not to remember how completely he had believed them, when he was a boy.

The sky was grey now, and the wind was picking up; it was hard to know whether the mist blowing into their faces was rain or spray from the waves. And when they heard a deep voice calling to them out of the mist, there was no knowing whether it came from an island or from a boat.

"Who is the master of this vessel?" called the voice. "Who speaks for the *Trout Queen*?"

Before David Macdonald or any of his crew could open their mouths, William Trout was yelling back.

"I am William Trout!" he boomed. "The Trout is master of the *Queen*!"

And so the deep voice of the Chief of the Blue Men called, through the wind,

> "Ship without sails, I challenge you here
> To follow my every rhyme!"

Trout gave an exasperated snort. "Who are you?" he yelled. "This is no time for games! Get out of our way!"

The wind howled louder, and a rogue wave caught the *Trout Queen* sideways so that her deck was suddenly aslant, sending Trout sliding across to the opposite rail. The sea was a mass of white-tipped waves; they seemed to break in all directions, leaving sudden holes that looked big enough to swallow up a boat.

Nessie and the Boggart were watching and listening in wonder.

The Chief of the Blue Men called once more:

> "Ship without sails, I challenge you here
> To follow my every rhyme!"

"Get us out of here, Macdonald!" yelled William Trout, clinging to the rail.

"*Yes!*" said the Boggart gleefully. "*Get him out of here, and make sure he doesnae come back!*"

But David Macdonald was a true Scottish sailor, and he had no intention of risking his ship, not even a ship that was the private toy of a self-centered billionaire. He thought very fast, and he decided that the stories of the Blue Men told by his long-dead grandmother were much more important than the orders of William Trout.

So he ignored his employer absolutely, and he called out to the Blue Chief, clear and loud:

"My ship and I, we have no fear,
And I'll match you every time!"

William Trout groped his way back across the deck, dripping. "Have you lost your mind?" he shouted.
The Blue Man called:

"My men are eagerly waiting now
To drag you below the waves!"

David Macdonald's imagination scurried round his head, hunting words. He called back:

"If you should sink my bonny ship
Its weight will crush your caves!"

"The boat's hardly moving, Macdonald!" bellowed William Trout. "Put up the speed!"
The Blue Chief called:

"Since you respect the Blue Men's way
I give you leave to pass!"

David Macdonald felt a great rush of relief that told him how frightened he had been, but still he had to find a rhyme. After a frantic few moments of groping, he called back:

"We give you thanks, and beg we may
Have seas as smooth as glass!"

He thought he heard a shadow of a laugh, as the sea mist swirled round the *Trout Queen*, but it was drowned out by the furious shouts of William Trout.

"What the hell do you think you're doing, Macdonald? Get us out of here, right now, or you're fired!"

Below the waves, the Blue Chief said a few words in Gaelic, his big voice filling the sea, and from the underside of the *Trout Queen* the Blue Men dropped away. Their long blue fingers let go of the keel, their hair swirled as they drifted down, down, and one by one they floated reluctantly into their caves, to wait for the next ship.

The Blue Chief drifted after them. He called to the Boggart and Nessie, in the Old Speech, *"I would have had your threatening man—but the Scot saved him."*

"I'm sorry he did," the Boggart said.

"Get rid of this man some other way, my friend," said the Blue Chief. His voice began to fade as he retreated into the blue glow of his cave. *"Try the Nuckelavee . . ."*

And he was gone.

Nessie said, *"The Nuckelavee?"*

"No, no," the Boggart said. *"Not that one. That fellow is a true horror. No."*

Above the surface, the wind eased a little, and the racing waves of the Minch seemed less threatening. The *Trout Queen* was moving again. David Macdonald steered as far away as he could from the Shiant Islands, where—his grandmother had said—the Blue Men had their caves. He felt his crewmen pass behind him, one by one, to give him murmured thanks and a grateful pat on the shoulder.

Clutching his way along the rail, William Trout came to join him.

"About time!" he said angrily. "Call yourself a captain— what do you think you were doing? Who was that guy? And what's with all the poetry stuff?"

David Macdonald looked at him, and wished once more that the previous owner of the boat now called the *Trout Queen* had sold it to somebody else.

"You could call it a local tradition," he said.

"Just remember who's in charge here," said William Trout. "And forget the golf course. Let's get out of this miserable place and go back to my loch."

TWELVE

Allie and Jay were cycling back from a meeting in the village called in support of their petition, which now had a gratifyingly large number of signatures. Their father and Granda were still there, headed for another meeting with members of the local council. The fight against Mr. Trout seemed to involve endless meetings and discussions and talking, and the only part the twins really enjoyed was their own current job: cycling to a house, knocking on the door, smiling brightly and offering the petition to just one person. They had been doing it for three days now and had managed to enlist Trout opponents of all ages. The older ones, they found, invariably did a double take, stared at them and cried, "You're Tommy's twins! You look just like him!"

Now they were pedaling up the last hill before the downward slope to the loch. Allie said to Jay, between puffs, "You think it really has a hope, this petition?"

"I dunno," Jay said.

"I'd rather be having a go at old Trout directly, like the boggarts. Even if it didn't work."

"So would I," Jay said. He stood up on his pedals, pumping

away to beat the last of the hill. "I wish we knew what's happening at the Minch."

And then neither of them said anything for a few moments, because they were over the hill, looking down at the place where the farm next door had been.

The farmhouse was a mound of rubble, and the gently sloping fields around it had become a flat stretch of dirt. Nearby, on the land where the two bulldozers had uprooted all the oak trees, the crane and the bulldozers were busily rumbling to and fro, pushing all the trees into a single huge pile facing Angus Cameron's store.

The twins slowed down, staring.

"Jeeze," Jay said. "Look at that!"

Allie suddenly found she had tears in her eyes. "It's like they dropped a bomb!" she said.

They saw Freddy the Site Manager, wearing his Trout Corporation jacket, talking to a group of men standing beside the road, near the pile of trees. One of the men was peering into what looked like a camera, set on a tripod. Another was planting a little orange flag into the ground some distance away. A third was a policeman, wearing a yellow-green vest over his black uniform.

"What are they doing?" Allie said.

Jay said, "This next field belongs to Granda, doesn't it?"

They walked their bikes closer, and Freddy looked up and saw them. He stopped talking, and the whole group paused, and stared at them. Freddy came toward them, frowning.

Allie said accusingly, "That's Granda's land, where you are."

"We're surveying," Freddy said. "Checking the boundary, between us and your grandfather."

He had a sheaf of papers in one hand, and a bunch of orange flags in the other. Allie and Jay looked at each other, remembering the orange ribbons they had removed from the trees marked to be cut down.

They also remembered that removing the ribbons had not saved the trees.

Jay said, "I thought people did surveys right at the very beginning."

Freddy was feeling irritable; he was having an annoying day and he mistrusted all the Camerons. He said curtly, "The original plans included your grandfather's land, back when we assumed he'd sell it, like any sane person. Now this whole part of the development has to be redesigned without it. So, a new boundary."

"Oh," Jay said.

"It's costing Mr. Trout a lot of money," said Freddy.

Allie looked at him coldly. She said, "He could save all his money if he just gave up the whole idea."

Freddy sniffed. "We know about that petition of yours," he said. "Waste of time. It's you guys who should give up."

Behind him an engine roared, and one of the bulldozers lurched toward them with its brimming jaw held high. It dropped a load of dirt on top of the pile of trees that faced Granda's store. Then a second bulldozer lumbered up and did the same. Then a third. A few lumps of the dirt rolled toward the surveyor who was planting the boundary line of orange flags, and he dodged out of the way.

The twins watched, baffled. One after the other, the machines lumbered off again toward the field from which they had collected their loads.

"They dug the trees up and now they're *burying* them?" Allie said.

Freddy studied the papers in his hand and ignored her.

Jay said, "That's crazy. It'll take a mountain of dirt."

Freddy smiled. It was not a nice smile. "That mountain will be called a berm. A berm is a barrier, in case you don't know. This one will save Mr. Trout's guests from having to look at your grandfather's store."

Allie burst out, "That's so mean!"

"It'll cut off half Granda's view," Jay said. "Like building a wall. I bet that's against the law."

"Oh no it's not," Freddy said. "You can check. And take a look, we have a police officer on duty now, in case anybody gets any funny ideas about interfering. Tell your grandad." He went back to his group and said something to the policeman, jerking his thumb toward the twins.

But the policeman, to the surprise of Freddy and the twins, too, immediately swung round and came toward them with his hand out, smiling. He was a medium-size man with a friendly, freckled face and curly red hair. "Well now!" he said. "If Angus Cameron's your grandad, you must be Tommy's babes!"

"That's right!" said Allie. She shook the hand, cautiously. "I'm Allie. Short for Alice."

Jay shook the hand too, as it swung toward him. "Jay," he said. "Short for James."

"I'm Ewan Nicolson," said the policeman. Unlike everyone

else connected to Mr. Trout, he sounded very Scottish. "I went to school with your dad! He was a lot brighter than me, mind. You look just like him!"

Allie said, "He's brighter than us, too."

"Is he here?" said Ewan eagerly.

"He's at a meeting, with Granda. We're working on a petition, to keep Mr. Trout from ruining Castle Keep and the whole loch!"

"Oh, aye," Ewan said uncomfortably. He hitched up his police vest.

"Would you like to sign it?" Jay said. "We've got one right here."

"Now come on, laddie—you know the law cannae take sides," Ewan said. He glanced across at Freddy, who had turned round to stare pointedly at him, and he sighed. "Remember me to your dad," he said. "We were good friends."

"I hope you won't have to arrest him," Allie said.

Ewan said, "Me too."

The Boggart and Nessie were coasting through the waters of Loch Linnhe long before the *Trout Queen* made its way back from the Minch. They were sorry that William Trout had survived the Blue Men, but not disheartened. Boggarts are by nature hopeful and persistent; they have survived for so many hundreds of years because their reaction to failure is not to give up, but to try again.

"*A council of war with our people, that's what we need,*" the Boggart said, as they wafted along the surface of the loch past the island of Shuna, a long, low, grassy place on the way to Castle Keep.

"What we need is to frighten the man away," Nessie said. *"The wee girl was right."*

"Well, ye canna try it again yoursel'. He loves the Monster—he's itching to see you back in the loch!"

"No, no, not me—we want something to make him run away. Like the Blue Man said: try the Nuckelavee!"

Not a yard ahead of them, a herring gull shot down into the water in pursuit of a passing fish, and the Boggart felt the terror of the fish even as it darted sideways and very narrowly escaped. The herring gull flapped up out of the loch and flew away, dripping, disappointed. The Boggart watched the fish unhappily.

"But the awful Nuckelavee, it hates the whole world!" he said. *"To let loose that horror, it'd be a dreadful thing! Let's go to our people, for a council of war. Like the old clan councils long ago, to decide what to do in battle."*

They passed a couple of elderly seals basking on the shore of Shuna Island, and the seals' whiskers twitched in greeting. They were fond of boggarts and their playful ways. Nessie felt the fondness, and lost all desire to argue; he cast about for a way to cheer his cousin up.

"There's your castle ahead," he said. *"We need to stop in, to tell it hello."*

"We do!" the Boggart said in relief, and he altered his course a little through the small waves. Centuries of MacDevon memories flickered through his mind, set in these waters round his favorite place in the whole world. They reached the castle, its grey, lichen-patched walls rising high from the rocky island, and with Nessie beside him the Boggart rose invisible, formless,

out of the water, looking down with disdain at the shiny new wood of the large new jetty added by William Trout. A chunky inflatable boat was tied up to it. In proper days, the Boggart thought nostalgically, it had been wee currachs made of hide that bobbed alongside the castle, not the noisy, smelly boats that brought the invading man and his people to and fro.

A window at the top of the castle was still open a crack, in spite of Freddy the Site Manager's stern instruction to his cleaning staff that the castle should be tightly shut against any kind of invasion, particularly from small creatures. (Before his departure for the Minch, William Trout had made him a short but very forceful little speech about cats.) The boggarts flittered in and made a silent, leisurely tour of the familiar corridors of the castle, pausing at the kitchen to sample the black-and-white American cookies now kept there in a jar as a snack for Mr. Trout. Then the Boggart made for the library, which for centuries had been the one place that his wandering, rootless mind came close to considering a home.

It looked different. The MacDevon's desk had been pushed into a corner and replaced by two tables, pushed together and lined with big chairs. The biggest chair was in the middle, high-backed, imposing, and was clearly intended for Mr. Trout, but in it now sat Freddy the Site Manager, his fingers pecking at a laptop computer. Piles of papers were stacked neatly on the table, and beside them, filling half its space, was the elaborate model of the Trout Castle Resort that had been shown at Trout's press conference. A second identically shaped model, hidden under a green canvas cover, filled another table nearby.

The Boggart suddenly felt a great longing to be at rest, in a familiar place still untouched by the influence of William Trout.

"*A nap, cuz,*" he said. "*It's still our home, they cannae change that—we'll take a wee nap.*"

So the two of them flittered up the library wall, to the space on a high shelf between two blocks of stone, and they dropped into a boggart sleep.

The parking lot beside Granda's store was a roaring mass of machinery, as bulldozers headed for the hillside and trucks were unloaded, inside the tall chain-link fence with its big notice CONSTRUCTION SITE: KEEP OUT. Pushing their bikes, Allie and Jay threaded their way through cars and cranes, past piles of wooden beams and metal spars. On the shore closest to Castle Keep, they saw an enormous pile of big rocks, some of them already arrayed at the edge of the water, to begin a causeway to the castle's island. In the few days since they had come back to Scotland, the tranquil shore had been utterly transformed.

They leaned their bikes against the side of the store, and went inside. Portia was there alone, behind the counter, making a list in a notebook. She looked up.

"Your mum rang from Canada!" she said. "You just missed her! She said she'd be on Skype for half an hour—go and ring her from Angus's computer."

"Great!" Allie said. "Granda and Dad aren't back yet?"

"Not yet," Portia said. "And not a soul has visited this store all day, except workmen buying soft drinks and chocolate bars. That Trout man claims he's bringing jobs to Scotsmen? Every one of this lot is an Irishman, with a couple of Americans."

Jay said, heading for the stairs, "Any sign of the boggarts?"

Portia laughed, and shook her head. "Who knows?" she said.

"Up the road, it's a disaster," Allie said. "They've pulled down the farmhouse, they've dug up every last tree."

"Better not tell your mother," Portia said.

And in a few moments, there was Emily Cameron on the computer screen, waving to them, more or less recognizable against a vague background of bookcases.

Before they could utter a word, she said, beaming, "Your dad says the boggarts are back!"

They stared at her. Here was a second parent suddenly admitting to this huge secret that they had never known. And on her face they could see the same mixture of delight and disbelief they had seen on the faces of Tom and Granda, when they first heard the Boggart's voice.

Allie said, "I can't *believe* you and Dad never told us about them!"

"You had the Boggart in *Toronto*?" Jay said.

"You'd never have believed it, and it was a long time ago," Emily said briskly, but she couldn't stop the smile from spreading over her face again. "We thought they'd gone away, him and Nessie. We'd almost felt we made them up—but they're back! It's wonderful! Just in time to help!"

"I don't know," Allie said. "They have some weird ways of helping, and nothing's stopping William Trout—he's wiping out the hills, he's taken over the castle—it's awful, Mom!"

Jay said hopefully, "Are you giving Dad and Granda legal stuff to stop him?"

"I'm trying," said Emily. "But listen." She leaned closer, and on the screen her eyes looked very big. "I have to go to a meeting in a minute—listen. You have to remember two things. One, you guys are really important in this, because you have MacDevon blood. Your Dad doesn't, Granda doesn't, but you do. From my dad, from his grannie—you two are the last pieces of the MacDevon clan. So you have to do anything you can think of to stop William Trout from hurting Castle Keep. It was the home of the clan for hundreds of years, it's soaked in pride and honor and loyalty, and he can't buy that even if he buys its walls. The Boggart knows that, and Trout can't buy the Boggart either. Or Nessie. They'll do anything they can to help you. You just have to stir them up."

"They are helping," Allie said. "They will. The trouble is . . . finding the right kind of help."

Outside the part-open window there was a loud and then fading roar as a bulldozer drove away, and a little gust of air blew in and ruffled the papers on Granda's desk.

Jay said, "What's the second thing?"

"Two: remember the Boggart's ways," their mother said. She paused, and her face softened, remembering. "Boggarts aren't like us. They're like light, or music, they're . . . well, they're *joy*."

Allie and Jay gazed at her. These were not the kind of words they usually heard from their practical lawyer mother, but they knew exactly what she meant.

"They can be very fierce about something that matters to them," Emily said, "but in the very middle of being serious they can switch, if they see some way of having fun. Their real thing in life is having fun, playing tricks. It's what they like best."

"Oh yes," Allie said. She thought of the boggart-seals pushing piles of wood into the loch, like gleeful children.

"But it doesn't mean they've forgotten—they do go back to what's important," Emily said. "So be patient. Have faith. Nudge them if you have to, but go along with the wacky things they do. It'll work out in the end." She looked at her watch. "Oh Lord, I have to go. I'll call you soon. Love to everyone, big hugs, I love you both."

"Love you too," said Allie.

"Wow those lawyers, Mom," said Jay.

Emily said, a little wistfully, "I'd say, give my love to the Boggart and Nessie, but they won't remember Jess and me. There's no space in their ancient heads. They don't attach themselves to people, just to the clan. That's all right, though. Good luck, my loves. Beat the Trout!"

She blew them a kiss, and she was gone.

Allie clicked out of Skype, and the screen of Granda's computer went dark.

But within its darkness they saw on the screen a gentle splash of light that was the touch of an invisible finger, and from the air of the room the Boggart's voice said softly, inquiringly, "Em-ily?"

Allie sat very still. She looked at Jay.

"Em-ily," said the Boggart. From a windowsill on the other side of Granda's office, a small picture frame rose into the air, traveled toward them and put itself down next to the computer screen.

"Em-ily," said the Boggart happily. "Jess-up."

They looked at the picture in the frame. It was an old photograph of their mother, aged about thirteen, with her younger brother, Jessup: their computer-whiz Uncle Jess, who ran an incomprehensible but highly successful company in Northern California with his partner, Barry.

"That's right, Boggart," Allie said. "That's them."

For a moment the Boggart made his sound that was like the purring of a cat, and then he said, in the same soft voice, "Al-lie. Jay."

Jay said, "That's right too, Boggart. Family."

Portia's voice rang up the stairs from the kitchen; she sounded excited. "Jay! Allie! Come on down!"

Allie put the computer to sleep and stood up. She looked round the room and its empty air, and she smiled. Then she followed Jay down the stairs.

The kitchen was empty too, but the door to the store was open; they went in, and found Portia, laughing, pointing to the ceiling.

A bright yellow balloon was hanging there, one of the helium balloons that Granda kept in stock for the smallest castle-visiting tourists. But though the other balloons hung in a still group at one end of the ceiling, this balloon was out in the middle on its own, and it was dancing. One-two-three, it hopped in one direction, bouncing off the ceiling, and then one-two-three back again. Very faintly, they heard a voice humming "Bonnie Dundee."

"We've got a boggart in a balloon," Portia said cheerfully. "I just don't know which one it is."

Jay said, "Hi, Nessie!"

The balloon gave a little extra bounce—and then in the air they heard the Boggart's husky chuckle, and a second balloon came sliding across the ceiling to join it, from the still cluster above the store's tourist-gift shelves. This balloon was a delicate shade of blue, and it joined in the dance. One-two-three, one-two-three they went, two voices humming now, until they ended the tune. Then each balloon hung there motionless, its string hanging down.

The twins and Portia clapped, and the two balloons gave a little bow, bending at mid-string.

"Thank you!" Allie said, laughing.

"It's like Mom said just now," Jay said to Portia. "Whatever else is happening, however important it is—if they see a chance to have fun, it's the fun that they'll choose."

"Sometimes I wish I'd lived all my human life that way," Portia said.

"But Boggart," Allie said, "tell us, tell us, what happened at the Minch!"

A long breathy sigh filled the room, and the blue balloon drooped.

The Boggart said, slowly finding the words, "We have tried, but it is hard to frighten the invading man. It will take all of us. We must all work together, we must have a council of war."

"Granda and Dad aren't here right now, they're at another kind of council," Allie said. "Also trying to drive him out."

"We tried too," the Boggart said. "Nessie tried. But the invading man laughs at the Loch Ness Monster. He wants it for a show."

Nessie said crossly, "He is not a natural man."

"And our wisest Old Thing the Caointeach sent us to the Blue Men of the Minch, but they had no chance to change his mind," the Boggart said.

"She did her best," Nessie said.

Both balloons nodded up and down, slowly, solemnly.

"She did," said the Boggart. "We owe her a debt, which we must go back and pay."

Jay looked blankly at Allie and Portia, and the look said, *What on earth is he talking about?* He said, "What do you owe her, Boggart? Can we help?"

"Just tell us what to do, and when, and we'll do it," Allie said.

The other balloon gave a small bounce, and Nessie's softer voice said, "You can cook some bacon."

There was a short, stunned silence.

"*Bacon?*" Allie said.

The Boggart said, "And then we may need help to take it to her, in a boat."

Jay said, "Why can't you take it by magic?"

"That's rude, Jay," Allie said.

"No it's not. Boggarts are magic. Perfectly good question."

The yellow helium balloon shifted to and fro on the ceiling, and Nessie sounded embarrassed. "Ah," he said. "It might get damp, when we go through water to a waterfall."

"We owe it to the Caointeach," the Boggart said. "She has looked for an Old Thing to drive away the invading man—the Each-Uisge, the Blue Men of the Minch, even the Nuckelavee. None of those may be right, but she did try."

Allie blinked at this mouthful of Gaelic names, none of which she could understand.

"Well, Angus has plenty of bacon in the fridge," Portia said. "If it's in the cause of getting rid of William Trout and his bull-dozers, I'm sure he'd cook it till the cows come home."

From the parking lot outside the store there was another sudden roar, as a mammoth crane-topped bulldozer headed up the hill.

Nessie said from the air, suddenly tense: "The bull dozers!"

"The tree killers!" the Boggart said.

The blue balloon and the yellow balloon were very still for a moment—and then they whipped across the ceiling toward the open door, and were gone.

THIRTEEN

Ewan Nicolson was on duty at the Trout development site every day from dusk to dawn; his superiors had refused to provide full twenty-four-hour protection, even after a personal call from William Trout. He had arrived early that day and found himself embarrassed by meeting the Cameron grandchildren, against whom he was supposed to be guarding this unpopular site. *Well,* he thought, *nothing personal—it's my job. I don't choose what to do.* Now the sun had just set, in the long summer day of the Western Highlands, and Freddy Winter and his men had gone away for the night. Ewan was sitting in his white police car eating the sandwiches that were his supper, with occasional sips from a thermos flask of hot coffee to help him stay alert. The front windows of the car were partly open, to let in fresh air, and he was trying to watch for the tiny stinging midges that always came in with it. On the seat beside him was his dessert, which consisted only of an apple because his wife felt he was in danger of putting on weight. In the glove compartment of his car there were also two bars of chocolate, though his wife didn't know about those.

Ewan took a bite of his last chicken sandwich and chewed. Meeting those children had taken his mind back a very long way, to his first friend, Tommy Cameron. He was thinking about a day thirty years before, when he and Tommy had sung a song together at the party that is called in the Gaelic a *ceilidh*. And Tommy had done a Highland dance, light as a feather, while he, Ewan Nicolson, played the fiddle. That was back in the days when he was a good fiddler, for one so young. He was remembering the feel of the strings under the fingers of his eleven-year-old left hand when suddenly he realized what he was seeing now, at this moment, out of the car window, and he nearly choked on his sandwich.

Two large round balloons were bouncing in the air above the two bulldozers parked on the farmland now owned by the Trout Corporation. One balloon was yellow, the other blue. Each had a string stretched down tight beneath it, but nobody was holding the strings. And though there was no breath of a breeze blowing, the balloons then moved sideways to the new hill of dirt facing Angus Cameron's store, and bounced there as well.

Ewan Nicholson sat there frozen, watching.

The balloons moved down from the hill to the survey-ors' string of small orange flags that now stretched along the boundary between Trout and Cameron land. They paused, as if in thought. Then they began to bounce again.

With each bounce, each balloon paused—and a small orange flag rose from the ground and hovered in the air next to the balloon's tight, straight string. Then another, then another. The balloons moved along the boundary, and flag after flag rose, until two growing bunches of flags were moving along with them, hovering, as if held by invisible hands.

Ewan blinked, and shook his head. He reached for his thermos, poured a cupful of coffee and hastily drank it, staring out through the window. But the balloons were still there, moving along, collecting flags now from the edge of the hill of dirt on the Trout land. It was eerie, and he knew he was afraid. For the first time since he was very young, he was afraid of ghosts.

But he was a policeman, on duty, not a fiddle-playing small boy. He was an educated man, trained to believe in facts that could be seen and proved. So he took a deep breath, put down his sandwich next to his apple, and got out of the car.

He saw both balloons give a little extra bounce, as if in greeting.

Ewan heard himself give a little moan, but he forced his legs to walk toward the boundary line—which was no longer visible, since nearly all the boundary flags had now flown up one by one to join the two large bunches hovering ahead. He thought he heard a breath of laughter in the growing dusk, but he hoped he was imagining it.

He was almost in reach of the nearest balloon. Its string stretched down underneath it, taut, with the bunch of flags at its side. He looked at it in despair. This was not possible; he was dreaming, or losing his mind. He would lose his career in the police force, his wife, his children. Nobody in the world would believe what he was seeing at this moment.

He reached out to grab the balloon's string.

And just before he could touch it, the string went slack and the balloon rose out of his reach, drifting high into the air, with the second balloon alongside it. Like two leisurely shooting stars, yellow and blue, they floated up and up, out of sight, into the twilit sky. But the bunches of flags didn't go with them; they flew sideways, through the air, past his police car, toward the loch.

Ewan ran after the flags, groping. He thought he heard the soft laughter again. The two bunches of orange flags rose higher, and they too gradually disappeared, over the water of the loch, as though they were heading past Castle Keep to the Seal Rocks.

Ewan stood there for a long moment, and then he went back to his car. He climbed in, and instinctively reached to clasp his seat belt around him, as if it could keep him safe. Though he would be here on duty for hours yet, he started the engine, and felt a flicker of relief as the reassuring beams of light shone out through the growing darkness, showing him the cleared land and the hill of dirt. Perhaps he had imagined everything in these last few minutes; perhaps another cup of coffee would clear his foolish head.

He looked down at the seat beside him, for final reassurance from his thermos of coffee and his dinner.

The thermos was still there, but the apple and half-eaten sandwich had gone, and there was no sign of them anywhere in the car. Instead, next to the thermos on the front seat, he saw a single orange boundary flag.

Portia had gone home, and Granda and Tom were back from their meeting. They were not happy about the reports they had heard from the local council, and they too had stared in disbelief at the ruined land they had passed on the way home, and the great earth barrier beyond the house.

"He's working really fast," Granda said. "And he's lying, he'll nae keep all these promises he's made to the government. They really seem to believe what he says, about protecting the coastline—at the same time as he's covering the shore wi' stones, and changing the water patterns. There are salmon farms in this loch, mussel farms—what's to become of them? We have to get some hard facts, to show him up! The Boggart's right about needing a council of war."

"But they went off again—do they ever stay anywhere for more than five minutes?" Allie said. "The Boggart said we all had to work together, with what he calls the Old Things, and then off they both went, with balloons."

"It was us mentioning bulldozers," said Jay. "Made them shoot off like rockets. They hate the bulldozers even more than they hate Mr. Trout."

"I doubt they'll move a bulldozer this time," Granda said. "Not with the police watching."

"If I'd known that cop was Ewan Nicolson, I'd have stopped to say hi," Tom Cameron said. "Remember him, Da? Red hair. Played the fiddle."

"It's a long time ago," Granda said

They were all upstairs in his study, examining the book that the departed Mr. Mac had given him: *Hauntings of the Scottish Highlands and Islands.* Allie wanted to look up the Boggart's mysterious mouthful of Gaelic names, after failing to find them online, but was having no success in finding any of them here, either.

"The only trouble with Gaelic," she said, "is that nothing looks the same as it sounds. The Kane-chuch, he said. I think. But it's not here."

"Spelled Caointeach," Angus Cameron said. "Look under C. And the *ch* at the end sounds the same as the *ch* in 'loch.'"

Jay turned pages. "Here it is. A wailer, it says, a little woman whose cry, rising to a scream, warns certain clans of impending disaster or death."

"Good grief," said Allie. "And she's the one who wants bacon?"

They had explained the Boggart's odd request to Granda and Tom and been amazed by how calmly they accepted it.

"And that other name, Granda," Jay said. "He said it so quick, it sounded like Ech-ooshga."

"That's pretty close," Granda said, "but it's spelled Each-Uisge, and you'll find that it's a water horse, an awful dangerous creature. And didn't he mention the Nuckelavee? That one's even worse."

Allie had found it in the book, with a large and alarming drawing. "A terrible sea monster, half man and half horse but with the head of each, and *no skin*! Yuk! And the only thing that can stop it carrying you off is if it has to cross fresh water! Do you believe in all these creatures, Granda?"

Angus Cameron looked at her over his glasses. "Do you believe in boggarts?" he said.

There was a short pause.

"I see what you mean," Allie said.

"Once," Granda said, "long ago, I said, 'There's no such things as boggarts'—and the Boggart and Nessie took me up in the air with them, and I flew. Your mum would remember that."

"She would indeed," Tom said. "I certainly do."

Granda looked out of the window across the loch, into the shadowy evening sky, and he smiled. "It was wonderful," he said. "Just wonderful. I dream about it, once in a while."

Jay said, "You really *flew*?"

"Well, they were holding me, of course," Granda said. "One on each side. But there I was, up there in the sky, swooping over the loch like a bird."

He looked down at the book. "Most of the time we choose what we believe in," he said, "but sometimes it just comes to you and it says, 'Here I am.'"

"Like a voice over the loch speaking Gaelic," Allie said, "even though there's nobody there."

"Just like that," Angus Cameron said.

The *Trout Queen* was back in the loch next day, anchored in the deeper water beyond Castle Keep, and William Trout was angry. He had had a miserable boat trip instead of a game of golf, there had been no more sightings of the Loch Ness Monster, and now there was a new irritation as well. Freddy Winter had come aboard, reluctantly, to report the disappearance of all the marker flags put in place by the surveying team, and the Trout reaction had been even louder than he expected.

"*What's the matter with you guys?* You can't keep a construction site safe from a couple of whiny Scots and two kids?"

"We don't know for sure who did it yet," Freddy said.

"I thought you had a cop watching everything?"

"We did. We do."

"I'm calling the cop office right now. Then I'm going over there myself. You know what my time is worth? Do you have *any idea*?"

He had gone on like this for longer than Freddy cared to remember, all the way across in the *Trout Queen* dinghy, and now they were over on dry land, watching the bulldozers drop more loads of dirt on the growing hill, waiting for PC Ewan Nicolson to come on duty.

"We'll have to have the surveyors come back and do all the work again, to make sure it's legal," Trout said. "This is ridiculous. I should take it out of your salary. Where was the boundary line?"

"Right next to the berm." Freddy pointed to the hill. He added hopefully, "It's getting big enough, right? Cuts off the view of Cameron's store completely."

William Trout grunted, and then swung round as Ewan Nicolson's gleaming white police car came bumping across the field. He began bellowing as soon as the car door opened, repeating everything that several people had already bellowed at Ewan in the last few hours, from the chief superintendent on down.

But none of these people had seen what Ewan had seen, and nor had William Trout.

"This better be the last time!" Trout roared. "They took the markers off the trees, they pushed our lumber into the water, they wrecked a bulldozer—and now they've stolen the survey flags! They're vandals! Stop them!"

"We certainly will, Mr. Trout, once we find out who they are," Ewan said.

Trout snorted. "It's obvious who they are! Weren't you on duty here last night, Officer? Were you asleep?"

Ewan thought, *Oh, I wish I had been asleep. I wish it had been a dream.*

He said, "Members of the police force do not sleep on duty, Mr. Trout. I was wide awake, and I promise you I didnae see one single human being touch your marker flags."

Trout said, "So they waited for you to leave, and came out once you'd gone. You think they're stupid? Use your imagination, man. If you'd pretended to go, and then come back to check, you'd have caught them red-handed."

Ewan shook his head. "The flags were not taken by the Cameron family," he said. "I'm sure of it."

"Garbage!" said William Trout. "How can you be sure?"

Because I saw a ghost do it, Mr. Trout. Two ghosts.

"It's under investigation, Mr. Trout," Ewan said.

Trout glared at him. His face was flushed and angry, and his heavy eyebrows hunched together in a frown. "I'm gonna put a stop to this! I want those people watched where they live— I'm gonna have you outside that miserable store, so you'll see every time they leave, every place they go! So let's go! Right now!"

Ewan Nicolson sat motionless in his police car. He said stiffly, "I cannae make any change without instructions from the office, Mr. Trout."

"Well, you'll get them, believe me!" Trout swung furiously away from the car, and Freddy Winter hurried to keep up with him as he strode back down the road toward the loch and Castle Keep.

"And you!" William Trout said, switching his angry gaze toward Freddy. "I want you based with me in the *Trout Queen*, not stuck out of phone range inside the castle. Right now! I'm sick of having to use radio—I need to be able to text you, and I need you to be able to reach everyone else."

Freddy began to explain the complications of Wi-Fi and mountains, but Trout flapped an impatient hand at him. "Spare me," he said. "Just move to the boat."

Freddy had a sudden happy image of a comfortable yacht cabin, instead of his nights in lonely Castle Keep.

"With pleasure," he said. "I'll do it today. D'you want me to bring all the plans and the paperwork? And the models?"

"No, there's more room in that library. And it gets me out on the water, going to and from the castle. *Why* haven't we got a picture of the Monster yet?"

"I've got people watching, day and night," Freddy said. "Some onshore, some in boats going up and down the loch." He didn't mention that everyone he had hired had clearly thought it was a joke. He added, "And all their cell phones work."

"Well, hire more, farther up the loch. We *have* to get a picture! Offer them a hundred-pound bonus for the first shot. I can't believe my camera didn't pick it up. At least I have you and those two sailors as witnesses—you saw it!"

"Yes," said Freddy, who had been trying to forget the sight and smell of Nessie ever since. "But we can't prove it either."

"Soon we will!" said William Trout hungrily. "Very soon!"

FOURTEEN

A morning mist hung over the loch, masking the far shore. The sky was grey, the water was grey, and the air was still and cool. Jay sat at the bedroom window, looking out through binoculars at the *Trout Queen* and making a note every time a boat left it for the construction site. His notebook also had columns for the times of arrival and departure for all the workmen and their trucks and cars. He and Allie were groping for any detail that might contradict local government's persistent good opinion of William Trout, since their father and grandfather had woken up even gloomier than ever.

"They trust him," Granda had said despondently. "They believe him when he says he's going to bring jobs to Scotland, even though his construction folk working out there now were hired from Ireland, because they were cheaper!"

"He's nothing but talk," Tom Cameron said. "And he's so glib—it's how he makes his money."

"Facts, that's what we need," Granda said. "Facts to prove when he's lying. Except of course that he'd say they were fake."

Now the two of them were already busy at their computers again, reaching out to all their petition signers to form an online army called The Resistance, and tonight in Port Appin they would be videotaping a talk by an environmentalist about all the damage that the Trout Castle Resort was likely do to Argyll's creatures and land and sea. All the Camerons would be there; Allie was hoping to be allowed to help with the taping.

Outside, the daily rumble and roar of machinery began to rise again. The mist faded into the grey sky, and a fine rain began to fall. Jay went downstairs, and found Granda had come down from his office to make a cup of tea.

Allie was still asking questions about the council meeting. "Didn't any of them talk about the wildlife and the birds, last night, and the seals' breeding ground?"

"Oh aye," Angus Cameron said. "There's some good sound people—but not enough. Well, they're all good sound people, it's just that they're so glad of the jobs and the investment, they let Trout feed them promises with a spoon. They dinnae question. Not enough, anyway."

"What happens next?"

"We go on making noise. We go on asking them to reconsider. We try to find a helpful law—maybe the man tonight will help wi' that. We all turn up outside their next meeting, wi' placards."

"When's that?" Jay said.

"Three weeks from now," Angus Cameron said.

"But we shall have gone home!"

"And so much damage will have been done!" said Tom. "Even if there's a council vote to stop, which is by no means certain." He was sitting in a corner with his laptop, writing an impassioned article about coastal preservation that he hoped to send to the *Guardian*.

Granda said, "It's just what we knew would happen—he's deliberately working fast, to get a lot done." He sighed. "Where are our boggarts when we need them? Playing games with balloons isn't going to help a bit."

"Resting, perhaps?" Tom said. "They did go all the way to the Minch and back."

"The Old Things, the old ways," Granda said. "That Caointeach of theirs may have a better answer than any of us, in the end."

"They have to tell us when to cook bacon," Jay said.

Allie said suddenly, "I'm going to make cookies."

Her father grinned. "Of course," he said. Allie's two favorite occupations were cooking and photography; it was a family joke, back in Toronto, that her response to any major problem was to dive into the kitchen and bake cookies or cupcakes.

"Chocolate chip cookies," Allie said. "The Boggart might smell them and come running."

"You're in Scotland," said Jay. "Granda doesn't sell chocolate chips."

"That's okay," said his sister. "You're going to make the chips. Granda, can I have a hammer?"

And before long Jay was sitting on the kitchen floor with a large bar of dark chocolate from the store, broken into squares, enclosed in a plastic bag and wrapped in a dish towel. He spent an enjoyable ten minutes whacking it with a hammer, inspecting the pieces of chocolate for uniformity at intervals and eating any that looked too small.

Later that day, the kitchen counter was covered in cookies studded with large, irregular chocolate chips. They lay there on racks, cooling off. They smelled wonderful. Everyone was allowed two each, for a treat after lunch.

But there was still no sign of the Boggart or Nessie.

The rain faded away into damp air, but the air was warm. The twins went out to look for seals, none of which had been seen in their own part of the loch since the noise of Trout Corporation trucks and machinery began. They splashed through puddles and slithered over seaweed to a rocky promontory facing the Seal Rocks, but there was not a seal to be seen even there.

"No seals, no Boggart, no Nessie," Jay said.

Allie said, "I really was hoping the cookies might bring the boggarts back. Like when Granda made porridge that time. I mean, where the heck are they? When the Boggart said we should have a council of war?"

"Maybe we should have our own," Jay said. "Just you and me. Now."

Allie looked at him blankly. "What d'you mean?"

"Remember what Mom said? About being part of the MacDevon clan? I mean, we are, aren't we? So *we* should be doing something, besides all this petition stuff! But what?" Jay kicked at the nearest rock, as if it might help him find out.

Allie said, "She said the castle belongs more to the clan than to William Trout. Or for that matter, Sam Johnson."

"And we're the clan, what's left of it, and he's keeping us out."

"So let's go there! To the castle, when nobody's looking. Maybe that's where the boggarts are holed up."

"Tonight? Instead of the meeting?"

"Yup. While Dad and Granda are gone."

Jay thought for a moment, trying to come to grips with the vagaries of boggarts, whose emotions seemed to come and go as unpredictably as the breeze. He thought of his grandfather's dinghy, and of taking it across the water to the castle. The motor was too noisy, he thought; they would have to row.

"Granda's still got his castle key," he said.

Allie said, "Portia saw them take that big model over to the castle, after the press conference. She said they nearly dropped it in the water."

They looked at each other, grinning, knowing what they were going to do next, and they headed back along the rocks, past the Trout trucks, toward the store.

It was past sunset, though nobody had seen the sun that day. Granda stood in the living room, looking at them uncertainly. He said, "Quite sure ye dinnae want to come?"

"I'm tired," Allie said. She curled up in an armchair, like a sleepy cat. "I'd rather go to bed early. You and Dad will tell us everything he says."

Tom looked at her with concern. "You were all steamed up this morning about hearing this talk—what's different? You sick?"

"No, no," Allie said. "Just tired. There's been lots of meetings. I'd like to look at Mr. Mac's book again."

Jay said, "I'm a bit tired too. Besides, maybe the boggarts'll turn up."

Granda picked up his laptop. "Well, we'll not be too long. Two, three hours or so. Ye'll be all right?"

"Of course!" they both said.

And when the door closed behind their father and grandfather, they watched from the window until the car disappeared over the hill. They had already taken turns, earlier, watching the workmen leaving for home, and Freddy Winter's inflatable dinghy heading to the *Trout Queen* for the night. Now they pulled on their jackets, helped themselves to two flashlights from the store, and took down the enormous iron key to the castle that still hung from a nail above the door.

"We can't use the motor," Jay said. "Oars. The oarlocks are there too."

They knew where Granda kept the oars to his dinghy—they saw them every day, propped inside the garage right next to the place where they parked their bikes. Down to the shore they went, in the soft evening light, each twin clutching an oar. The loch lay calm and glimmering beyond the piles of lumber and machinery, and Granda's boat was moored at one end of a massive work jetty on which barges now regularly dropped steel beams and sacks of cement. He had argued bitterly with Freddy for the right to leave the boat there, and—for once— had had his way.

They had tossed a Canadian dollar to see who should row, and Allie had won. Jay sat in the bow, holding the line. As they crossed to Castle Keep, the water was so still that he felt even the small creak of the oarlocks was loud, but there was no other boat to be seen between them and the bright lights of the *Trout Queen*, farther up the loch. They could hear music pulsing faintly across the water.

"Light pollution, noise pollution," Allie said crossly.

"Of course. Trout doesn't care. And it's not even good music. . . ."

With the dinghy tied up to the castle's jetty, they climbed the steps and found, to their relief, that the lock in the heavy old door had not been changed. And the door still creaked, like the soundtrack to a horror movie—yet somehow managed to sound welcoming. Just inside, lying on the floor, they saw two untidy piles of orange flags, and thought hostile thoughts about Freddy Winter and the Trout Corporation surveyors.

They walked through the dark corridors, in a black world lit only by the small pale flickers of their flashlights, and they expected to feel scared but were not.

Allie said softly, "Hello, castle."

Jay called out, hopefully, "Boggart? Nessie?" But there was no answer.

They went up the stairs to the library, and played their flashlight beams over the unfamiliar long table that now lay where the MacDevon's desk had been. One end of it was filled by the big model of the Trout Castle Resort that they had seen at the press conference, draped now in its green cloth cover. From a plug lying on the center of the table, they could see a trio of little wires waiting for laptops or cell phones, and several folders and files of documents were stacked in front of the biggest chair.

"The invading man's seat, I bet," Allie said, and she sat herself in William Trout's chair and pointed her flashlight at the folders on the table, opening the first of them and peering at the papers inside. She pulled her cell phone out of her pocket and clicked its camera on.

Jay moved his flashlight beam sideways to the model of the Trout Castle Resort. He pulled back its cover and played the light over the sprawling modeled hotel, and the marina that reached out into the loch like a geometric octopus. In this model Troutworld, it was hard to guess where Granda's store had been.

From somewhere in the dark room he thought he heard a small, indistinct sound. He swung his flashlight to and fro, but he could see nothing in the shadows but the library's roomy armchairs and the bookcases lining the walls.

"What was that?" he whispered.

Allie clicked her camera at one of the documents on the table in front of her, making a small, quick flash. "I didn't hear anything," she said.

As Jay swung his arm back again, the flashlight beam caught out of the darkness another massive object on a table farther away. It was the same shape as the resort model, but it too was masked by a cloth cover. He moved over to it and carefully folded the cover back.

It was a copy of the first model—but with one startling difference. Castle Keep, the familiar square tower on its small green island, was not there.

In its place, on an immense stretch of stone reaching all the way to the island from the shore of the loch, was a much bigger structure with stone walls and battlements, and a tall round tower topped with a flagpole. It was separated by a channel of water from the boat-thronged marina of the resort, and it looked very much like pictures of Windsor Castle, in England—though with two little plastic flags flying from its model flagpole instead of the Union Jack. One was the Scottish red lion, and the other a black flag with a big yellow T in the middle.

Jay thought he heard another soft sound in the room, but he was too startled to pay it any attention.

"Look at this!" he said, aghast.

Allie turned in her chair, and stared. Then she jumped up and reached for one of the documents on the table in front of her. She held it out.

"That explains this!" she said. "It's a drawing labeled Castle Condominiums, and that—that . . . thing . . . is full of apartments. With all those fake battlement walls around it. There's a spa in the middle, a gym and a sauna and a hot tub, and a little swimming pool! I thought it was part of the hotel, but it's right there on that island. *He's going to pull down Castle Keep!*"

"He can't do that!" Jay said.

Allie said, "It's in a folder called 'Second Stage.'" She set the drawing next to the folder, and her camera flashed.

"Here, hold this," Jay said, thrusting his flashlight at her, and he pulled out his own phone and took pictures of the second model from several different directions.

"He's keeping it a secret till it's too late to stop him!" Allie said.

"Just wait till Granda sees this! Talk about evidence!"

Allie suddenly looked at her watch. "Come on," she said. "We have to go—Granda and Dad will be back soon."

So in a quiet flurry they pulled back covers and put papers

back into files, to leave the dark room just as it had been before they came, and they crept carefully out through the shadows, out of Castle Keep, back to the dinghy on the loch.

And in the MacDevon's library, where until ten minutes ago they had been fast asleep, the Boggart and Nessie hovered in silent shock, not speaking even to each other, trying not to believe the things that they had just seen. Things that would finally drive their clannish souls to seek their own weapon of war.

FIFTEEN

Allie scrambled out of the dinghy and held it against the tall side of the new jetty, as Jay climbed out with the oars. A small wind had sprung up now over the loch, and the cloud cover above them was broken, so that they could see separate clouds moving through the almost-night sky. Ahead, they could see the lights of the house, and a car moving down the road toward them—but it wasn't their father, it was a white police car, shining even in the darkness.

They paused, and so did the car. Ewan Nicolson opened his window and looked out at them. "Ah," he said. "Ah—good evening."

"Hi," Allie said. "Granda's not here."

"I'm not here tae see him," Ewan said. He looked oddly embarrassed, for a policeman. "Ah—I'm on duty for the night, out here. All night, every night, now. Request from Mr. Trout."

"All night?" Allie said.

Ewan said hastily, "I'll park myself out of the way, you'll not have tae look at me. Don't worry!"

And he drove slowly down to the shore of the loch, where

the water glimmered in the almost-dark, and made his way round a stack of big stones.

"'Request from Mr. Trout!'" Jay said witheringly. "He wants a cop out here in case we come out in the middle of the night and pull up his concrete posts? Give me a break!"

"Poor man," Allie said, looking after Ewan. Then she looked farther away. "Hey, let's get rid of these oars—there's another car coming, it might be Dad."

Headlights were coming down the hill. They hurried to the garage, and they had just propped their oars back against the wall when Tom's car came to a halt next to Granda's elderly Land Rover. Jay pushed the garage door shut as his father got out of the car.

"What are you two up to?" Tom said. "I thought you were both so tired."

"Just checking," Jay said vaguely.

"How was the talk?" Allie said.

"Excellent," said Granda. He strode into the house, reporting on the scientist's predictions of environmental disaster as he went, and the twins listened for several minutes before the news bubbling inside their own heads had to burst out of them.

Tom was saying to Granda, "But Trout will deny it all, that's the problem. He'll say there's no proof, he'll say, 'My intentions are wonderful—'"

Allie pulled out her cell phone and held it up. So did Jay. "Look!" he said. "Here are Mr. Trout's real intentions!"

"We got you some facts, Granda!" Allie said triumphantly. "Look at what he's planning to do to Castle Keep!"

And there was a prickling silence, as Tom and Angus

Cameron stared at the plans and the pictures of William Trout's second stage of development.

Tom gave a long, slow whistle.

"Dear Lord!" Granda said.

"Is it illegal?" Jay said hopefully.

"Well, Castle Keep is historic, so it's a listed building," Tom said. "Which means you can't change it in any way without asking permission from the local authority."

"Which they'll not give," said Granda, "not when they see this! And maybe it'll be the thing that finally turns their minds about Mr. Trout an' his whole resort." He reached out both arms and hugged the twins. "Well done, wee MacDevons! First thing tomorrow, this goes to the council!"

"Tomorrow's Saturday," Tom said.

"So it is. Well, first thing Monday!"

"Couldn't we put his plans online?" Annie said. "Now?"

"I wouldnae do that—let's not give Trout any warning, to dream up lies and excuses. Best for the council to spring it on him." Granda opened the pantry door and took out a bottle of whisky. "The grown-ups'll toast ye!" he said.

Tom said, "And even more important than the council, the Boggart has to see these pictures! When did you take them?"

"The model's in the castle library," Jay said evasively. "All Trout's planning stuff is there."

Their father was turning to the kitchen sink, with the kettle in his hand. He paused, frowning. "You went over there tonight?" he said. "You took the boat over? In the dark?"

"It wasn't *very* dark," Jay said.

"You should have asked," Tom said.

"We were very careful," said Allie. She had a sudden inspiration. "We saw that friend of yours, the policeman! He's out there in his car, now, he has to stay all night. Mr. Trout wanted someone on duty."

"Against vandals like us," Jay said.

Granda said something short and explosive in Gaelic.

"But he's nice, the cop," Allie said. "It's not his fault."

Tom Cameron stood there holding the kettle, his face softened by memory.

"Ewan Nicolson," he said. "Oh my. I should go out there and say hello."

Allie said, "I could take him some cookies."

"And maybe a thermos of tea," Granda said. "Quite true, it's no' his fault, poor soul. Maybe a blanket, too, in case it gets chilly."

A small flurry of activity began in the kitchen, and Jay opened the door and looked out. Out on the loch, behind the familiar silhouette of Castle Keep, the *Trout Queen* lay at anchor, strung all over with lights like a fairground carousel, but on their own shore, beyond the machines and the piles of planks, he could just make out the glimmer of the police car's white hood. He thought he could hear a voice, murmuring very faintly.

"He's still there," he said.

In his car, Ewan Nicolson heard the door of the house close, and he sighed, feeling isolated. For the sake of his car's battery, he turned off the player on which he had been listening to an audio version of Stevenson's *Kidnapped*, though David

Balfour eating raw limpets had been a welcome distraction from the thought of William Trout. At least the rain had stopped. He looked out; through the broken clouds he could see a sliver of moon now, and two or three bright stars in the darkening sky.

And then the door over at the Cameron store opened again, and he saw a group of figures walking toward him. He sat up, warily, and opened the car window. One of the figures came closer.

"Ewan Nicolson!" Tom said.

Ewan's face changed as if a light had been turned on inside it. He fumbled with his door handle and almost fell out of the car. "Tommy!" he cried. "Tommy Cameron!" He thrust out his hand, and they pumped fists for a moment; then they both laughed and gave each other an awkward hug.

The twins watched their father's transformed face, fascinated.

Ewan smiled at them and reached out his hand to Granda. "Mr. Cameron, sir," he said.

"Evening, Ewan," Granda said.

Ewan gestured helplessly at the Trout Corporation construction site, and at his car. "I'm sorry about all this," he said unhappily.

Allie handed him a plate.

"I made Canadian cookies," she said. "We thought you might like some."

"Thank you!" said Ewan, astonished.

"And hot tea," said Granda, handing him a thermos. "Wi' a dram added."

"Oh!" said Ewan gratefully. Then, with an effort, he shook his head. "I cannae have whisky, not on duty," he said.

"Ah, it's mostly tea," Angus Cameron said, "and who's to know whether I lied? Just drink it, man."

"Mr. Cameron, you are a gentleman," said Ewan. "And duty or no duty, I want you to know that I signed your petition. Not as a policeman, you understand. As a Scot."

"I'm proud of you," Granda said.

"You're all very kind," Ewan said. He put the tea and the plate of cookies on the seat of his car, and then took one of the six cookies and bit into it. "Mmm!" he said.

It was Jay who saw one of the other cookies on the plate instantly disappear.

"Boggart!" he said.

Another cookie vanished.

"*Nessie!*" said Jay.

"What?" said Ewan Nicolson. Chewing, he failed to notice the soft flicker of laughter that the others could hear.

"Nothing," Jay said. "Hi. I'm Jay."

"I remember," Ewan said. "Short for James. Your sister is a good cook." He glanced down at the plate and blinked uncertainly, seeing only three cookies where he thought there had been more.

Tom said, hastily, loudly, "So they've got you here to stop us knocking down the new jetty!"

"They're back!" Jay hissed to Allie. "Finally!"

"They are! We have to talk to them! It's urgent!"

They both looked at Ewan Nicolson and wondered what to do.

Ewan took the thermos of tea out of the car and opened it. "Orders is orders, Tommy," he said. "No matter how daft."

"They're certainly that," Tom said.

"And getting dafter," Ewan said. "I hear they're bringing in a dredger next week, to dig out the loch bottom for his new marina."

"You're not serious!" Granda said. "We were hearing the council last night, but they didnae mention that."

"Oh aye. He's got all his permissions, even from Conservation. Convinced them again that it's jobs for Scotsmen, an' all that." Ewan took a swig from his thermos and held it out to them. Gloomily they each took a large swallow.

From the jetty, there was a shifting sound as the work boats moved a little, even though there was not a ripple on the silent loch, nor any breath of wind.

"Did you hear that?" Nessie said to the Boggart. *"Before the invader knocks down the castle, he's digging up the loch!"*

"I never heard worse," the Boggart said miserably. He was back again in the fear that had swamped him in the library, as the twins uncovered the invader's plan to demolish Castle Keep. *"And there's only one Old Thing left who can help. I should have the Caointeach send him to us, I should, I should. But he's such a horror, the Nuckelavee, how can I loose him on the world?"*

Tom said, "This could never have happened when the MacDevon was alive."

Granda nodded. "When he spoke, everyone listened—even when he was older than I am now."

Ewan took another swig of his tea. "Remember when he had that *ceilidh* at the castle, Tommy? You and me went together.

We were a big hit, even though we were so young. I doubt I've been inside it since."

Tom Cameron said to the twins, remembering, "Ewan played the fiddle and I danced. And then we sang. Our voices hadn't broken yet."

Jay stopped thinking about the Boggart for a moment. "Which song?" he said.

"The one making fun of the English general."

"'Hey Johnnie Cope,'" Ewan said.

"That's it."

"I know that one!" Jay said. "I've sung it!" He stood still suddenly and remembered performing for a competition at home in Canada, where the bouncing tune had enchanted people even though they couldn't understand half the Scots-English words.

And perhaps because he was in Scotland and not Canada, perhaps because he had no public audience, perhaps because Castle Keep lay shadowy before him in the loch—Jay Cameron began to sing.

> *"Cope sent a challenge frae Dunbar,*
> *Sayin' 'Charlie meet me if ye dare;*
> *An' I'll learn ye the art o' war,*
> *If ye'll meet me in the morning.'"*

He reached the chorus, and Tom joined in. So did Ewan, clapping his hands on each beat.

> *"O hey! Johnnie Cope, are ye waukin' yet?*
> *Or are your drums a-beating yet?*

If ye were waukin' I wad wait,
Tae gang tae the coals in the morning."

Jay sang on, facing the water, ignoring the Trout Corporation machinery around him. The thin sliver of moon hung clear now in the cloud-patterned sky, reflected below in the loch, and more stars were beginning to prickle here and there. From where he stood, the lights of the anchored *Trout Queen* were almost hidden by the dark outline of the castle and its island.

"When Charlie looked the letter upon,
He drew his sword and scabbard from,
Come, follow me, my merry men,
And we'll meet Johnnie Cope in the morning."

This time Granda joined in the chorus too, and so did Allie, picking it up as she went along. They sang at the tops of their voices, joining Ewan and Jay and Tom, a happily ragged choir.

"O hey! Johnnie Cope, are ye waukin' yet?
Or are your drums a-beating yet?
If ye were waukin' I wad wait,
Tae gang tae the coals in the morning."

And the Boggart and Nessie, insubstantial in the night air, flickered joyfully to and fro, scarcely able to believe what they were hearing.

"It's a song for Prince Charlie again! And it's our people singing it!"
"A fighting song!"

"A song for this fight of our own!"

Like a conductor, Jay pointed at Ewan and beckoned to him with one finger for the next verse. And Ewan's deep voice rang out alone, with the words of Charles Edward Stuart, the Young Pretender, leading his invading troops to try to take back his grandfather's throne of Britain from the German-born English King George.

> *"Now Johnnie, be as good as your word,*
> *Come, let us try both fire and sword,*
> *And dinna flee like a frightened bird,*
> *That's chased frae its nest i' the morning."*

They all roared into the chorus, and every one of them knew, even Police Constable Ewan Nicolson, that they were calling for the defeat not of long-dead enemy General Sir John Cope, but of their very much alive enemy William Trout.

> *"O hey! Johnnie Cope, are ye waukin' yet?*
> *Or are your drums a-beating yet?*
> *If ye were waukin' I wad wait,*
> *Tae gang tae the coals in the morning."*

Ewan in turn pointed a finger at Jay, and Jay took up the song again, gleefully reaching the verse about the cowardice of the enemy.

> *"When Johnnie Cope he heard o' this,*
> *He thocht it wouldna be amiss,*

Tae hae a horse in readiness,
Tae flee awa in the morning."

And they all threw themselves into singing the chorus with such vigor that it was a while before they noticed the music that was beginning to overlay their own music: they heard the sound of bagpipes, faint but growing, and behind it other distant voices, and the defiant regular beat of a drum. The sounds grew, unmistakable, and they looked at one another in wonder as they sang.

"O hey! Johnnie Cope, are ye waukin' yet?
Or are your drums a-beating yet?
If ye were waukin' I wad wait,
Tae gang tae the coals in the morning."

Then Ewan's voice was singing alone again, and every one of them—Tom, Angus, Allie, Jay—wondered whether they had really heard the bagpipes and the drum, or whether the drama of the song had produced the music out of their imaginations.

"Fye now, Johnnie, get up an' rin,
The Highland bagpipes mak' a din,
It's better tae sleep in your own whole skin,
For it will be a bloody morning."

But when they were back at the chorus, the bagpipes were as loud and clear as if a line of pipers stood along the shore; and this time a chorus of men's voices was growing along with their own, shouting the words into the night air. They knew this was the Boggart's doing, and they neither knew nor cared how he was doing it, as the music picked them up and carried them, as the past reached forward and caught the present into its wake.

> "O hey! Johnnie Cope, are ye waukin' yet?
> Or are your drums a-beating yet?
> If ye were waukin' I wad wait,
> Tae gang tae the coals in the morning."

Jay was back at singing the story, and he had never enjoyed a song so much in his life before. They were all standing around him now, caught up in its scorn for the unfortunate English general and his men. Jay's clear soprano voice pealed out into the darkness.

> "When Johnnie Cope tae Dunbar cam,
> They speired at him, 'Where's a' your men?'
> 'The de'il confound me gin I ken,
> For I left them a' in the morning.'"

As the pipers and the voices roared out the chorus, the Boggart and Nessie whirled with delight, and though boggarts are not commonly known to sing, they were singing too, lost in the music and the scorn that was their defense of their own place.

> "O hey! Johnnie Cope, are ye waukin' yet?
> Or are your drums a-beating yet?

If ye were waukin' I wad wait,
Tae gang tae the coals in the morning."

And while the air above the Camerons and Ewan Nicolson was filled with a great wave of sound from singers and players who were not there, each of them saw now too an eerie, beautiful shifting of color and light through the air, which was the nearest they would ever come to seeing the true form of a boggart. Magic had hold of them. They all found themselves singing together, singing words aimed at the enemy of the present day, the enemy behind the tiny strings of lights decorating the outline of the *Trout Queen.*

"Now Willie Trout you were not late
To come with the news of your own defeat,
And leave your men in such a strait,
So early in the morning.

O hey! Willie Trout, are ye wakin' yet?
And are your drums a-beating yet?
If you were wakin' I would wait
And wave you good-bye in the morning!"

They gave a last shout, and the triumphant bagpipes and voices left an echo hanging over the loch and the mountains beyond. It was like a marching song, and it caught the Boggart up into a passionate determination to march every Old Thing, even the one who was a horror, on a crusade to defeat their enemy.

"*Now!*" he cried out to Nessie. "*Now we have to go after him! We're at war! And if it takes the calling of the Nuckelavee, that's what we'll do! We'll call it up! We have to go back to the Caointeach right now!*"

Then he remembered his people, around him there on the shore of the loch, and he called out the same thing again, not in the silent Old Speech but in his hoarse Scottish English. The heads went up in excitement as they all heard his voice, and he knew the crusade was theirs too.

"We're with you, Boggart!" Jay yelled.

"Whatever it takes!" Tom Cameron called.

Nessie's voice said from the air, "Gi'e us bacon!"

"Absolutely!" Granda said. "First thing in the morning, I promise!"

"No," the Boggart called. "Now! Now this minute!"

Ewan Nicolson said helplessly, "Bacon?"

They had all forgotten about Ewan. Tom Cameron looked at the utter confusion on his face and knew that explanations would be far too much.

"Boggart?" he said into the air. "Nessie? This is our friend Ewan Nicolson, who is a policeman but who thinks as we do."

"And he's a gey good singer," the Boggart said, "even if he cannae catch balloons."

Ewan Nicolson stood there listening to the disembodied voice. They watched his face go from disbelief to remembering, to understanding, to more disbelief, to a surrendering acceptance. He began to smile. He said to Tom, "I'll tell you about the balloons if you tell me about the bacon."

"I'm away to cook it," Granda said. "Do you want some?"

"I'm on duty," Ewan said. "And there's nae word at all in my report about tonight, nor will be, even though I've heard things I'll not forget if I live to be a hundred and ten."

The Boggart and Nessie whirled impatiently round the kitchen above Granda's head, as he stood at the stove with a skillet filled with sputtering slices of bacon. He felt a slight draft lift his white hair.

"It cannae be rushed," he said. "Not unless you want me to burn it."

Allie said, to the air, "Are you sure it should be streaky, not back bacon?"

"Crisp and crunchy, she said," said the Boggart.

"That's right then," said Jay. He sniffed enviously. "Sure smells good, Granda."

"We are absolutely not having breakfast at ten o'clock at night," said his grandfather. With a fork, he lifted two slices of bacon from the pan to a waiting paper towel. "Just one piece each for the messengers."

The bacon instantly vanished, and he smiled. Then he began lifting out all the other pieces and setting them to drain.

"But it's too late at night for the boat, Boggart," Tom Cameron said. "So unless you can wait till the morning, you and the bacon are on your own."

"We figured out how to keep it crisp, though," Allie said. "And waterproof. Granda had just the right thing." She produced a translucent plastic container, and began layering bacon and paper towels into it until it was full. Then she snapped on its plastic lid, and she held it up in the air.

She felt a little tug, and the plastic box was gone.

There was an emptiness in the room, and they knew that the boggarts had gone too.

"Well," Granda said, "here's hoping the Old Things can get Willie Trout to fly away like a frightened bird."

"With bagpipes playing," said Jay.

SIXTEEN

Their quest to the waterfall of the Caointeach took the bog-garts longer this time, since they were carrying something solid, real and—unlike them—visible. The darkness hid what would have been an alarming sight to a stranger: a plastic box moving mysteriously unsupported over the small waves of the loch, slowly but with determination.

It was the magical time between dawn and sunrise when at last they turned inland to reach the tall grey rocks where the river fell and splashed. There was no rainbow over the water-fall yet, and the air was cool.

The Boggart called to the Caointeach, and very gradually she took shape, sitting there on a wet grey rock. Her green skirt spread down into the water with little color in it yet, and her tall white cap glimmered in the slowly growing daylight.

"You again?" she said. *"What is it this time?"*

"We kept our promise," Nessie said.

"We brought you this," said the Boggart, and he put the box carefully into her lap.

The Caointeach took off the lid. She raised the box to her face, and sniffed. She made a soft noise like crooning, and she took out a first piece of bacon between her finger and thumb and popped it into her mouth. They noticed for the first time that she had six fingers on each slender hand.

She crunched.

The Boggart said anxiously, *"We tried to keep it crisp."*

"Aaah," said the Caointeach ecstatically. She ate several more pieces of bacon, taking her time, making small happy noises between bites. Then she put the top back on the box and stowed it carefully away in the voluminous folds of her skirt.

She smiled at them. *"It's been a very long time,"* she said, *"but it tastes even better than I remembered. Thank you."*

"Our people sent it, with their good wishes," the Boggart said.

In a gradual dazzling blaze, the sun rose over the horizon beyond the rocks, and the sky was more blue and the Caointeach's skirt glowed a brighter green. She said, still blissful, *"What can I do for them?"*

The Boggart took a deep breath. *"You can summon the Nuckelavee,"* he said.

The Caointeach stopped smiling. She said, *"Do they know what they are asking?"*

Nessie said firmly, *"We are asking it too, Caointeach."*

"We are at war," the Boggart said. *"Nothing else has put fear into our enemy, and he has to be driven out. We know now that he will destroy our castle. It is time for the Nuckelavee."*

The Caointeach said, *"You do understand that it can be summoned by an Old Thing, but not controlled? That it has a passionate hatred for all human beings and is more dangerous than anything else in the wild?"*

"This one human being has no respect for any of the rest," said

the Boggart. *"He needs a sight of the Nuckelavee, to show him that he cannae stay here!"*

"Very well then," the Caointeach said, though she still sounded a little reluctant. *"It is a creature of the sea, so you must go to the salty loch."*

She stood up, planting her bare feet squarely on the rock. *"I will meet you at the first bay that is north of my river,"* she said, and suddenly she was gone.

The Boggart and Nessie wafted themselves back to the loch, over the river, over the green hills, looking down. There she was, on a beach that was more rock than sand, standing just as she had a little while before. The water of the loch stretched all around them, unpopulated by boats or people so early in the morning. They flittered down and hovered beside her.

"Very well," said the Caointeach. She took a deep breath. *"Keep at a distance, my friends. Give it some space. I have to bring it here all the way from Orkney, and it will not be pleased."*

The Boggart and Nessie flowed away from her like a small gust of wind, and hovered, watching.

The Caointeach stood very still, with her eyes closed, and they saw her lips moving, though they could hear nothing that she said. There was a faint humming in the air, and for a moment the sunlight seemed to die.

Then, with a shock like a soundless thunderclap, something huge was suddenly there.

It stood with its feet in the water. It was hideous. The body was like a gigantic horse, but with flaps of skin like fins around its legs, and its head was split by a mouth as vast as a whale's, wide open, gusting out evil-smelling breath like clouds of steam.

The head had only one eye, a great red eye in the middle of the forehead. And out of the back of the horse grew the top half of an enormous legless man, with arms so long that they nearly touched the ground. It was a centaur from a nightmare. The fingers of the hands clenched to and fro, to and fro, grasping at nothing, and the man's head was five times as big as the head of a normal man, on a neck that rolled endlessly sideways across the shoulders to and fro, to and fro, as if it were trying to roll off.

The Boggart and Nessie backed away, still invisibly hovering, and they saw that the worst horror of the Nuckelavee was that it had no skin. The double body of the man-horse was all raw flesh, red and naked, streaked with yellow veins through which the blood ran black, and between and across the veins were muscles like thick white ropes, twisting and swelling as the creature moved.

The Nuckelavee looked at the Caointeach and it reared up, snarling. From the great horse-mouth its foul breath poured out in a grey cloud, past rows of jagged yellow teeth. Its voice came out of its man-head and was loud, grating, slow.

"What do you want?" it said.

The Boggart called down, *"Your presence, is all! We are honored!"*

The Nuckelavee stared at the air with its three eyes, puzzled.

"What do you want?" it roared.

The Boggart wondered if it needed to see him, but he couldn't think of a suitable shape to take. Still formless, he flittered down closer to the Nuckelavee—though not too close.

"We want you to show yourself to someone," he said. *"To frighten him. Please."*

The Nuckelavee was not accustomed to disembodied voices, and the ears of its upper head did not hear very well, perhaps because of the constant sliding from one shoulder to the other. It gave another terrifying, uncomprehending roar.

"*I have an idea,*" Nessie said. "*Let me try!*" And in an instant he was no longer an invisible formless boggart, but down in the waves in his Loch Ness Monster form. His massive body was half-submerged in the deeper water beyond the Nuckelavee, and his long neck towered over its two heads.

"*Old Thing!*" he called. "*Come swim with me!*"

The Nuckelavee's upper head looked surprised, through all its ugly network of veins and muscles. It stared at Nessie, and stopped swinging to and fro for a moment.

"*Come on!*" Nessie called. He bent his neck, dived down and came up again, dripping. "*It's fun! I'll race you!*"

"*Nobody has fun with the Nuckelavee!*" said the rusty voice flatly.

"*Well, not humans, I'm sure,*" Nessie said.

"*I kill them!*" bellowed the Nuckelavee. "*And I kill their cows and their horses and their dogs! I hate them all!*"

"*But come swim with an Old Thing!*" Nessie called cheerfully. "*With the Monster from Loch Ness, who has never seen another monster before!*"

He did his dive again, and shook spray from his doglike head over the Nuckelavee as he came up.

The Nuckelavee took a few paces into deeper water on its strange finned legs. The only voices it remembered were howls of terror, or screams for mercy; it didn't know how to cope with Nessie.

From the air, the Boggart watched, fascinated.

Nessie plunged his long neck into the water and swam round in an enormous circle. Only the top of his head was visible, and then the hump of his great body, and behind it the flailing of his powerful tail. When he came back to the Nuckelavee, he raised his head long enough to give an exuberant hoot, like a long-ago railroad train, and then he set off again.

And after a moment, the Nuckelavee ducked into the water and followed him. It plunged both its heads into the loch, and it swam completely submerged, never coming up for air; only the swirling of the water showed where it was going. But whenever Nessie paused to surface, the Nuckelavee paused too, and though it never uttered any sound like Nessie's amiable chortle, it seemed to have decided to trust him.

After a third circle, Nessie changed direction and headed for the opening where the loch joined Loch Linnhe, and Castle Keep, and the *Trout Queen*. The swirl of water that was the Nuckelavee followed him, and the Boggart, watching, grinned in admiration.

"Come on, cuz!" Nessie called. *"We're on our way!"*

The Caointeach had been watching too. It was a very long time since she had last felt called to fulfill her other traditional task, the warning of certain clans when disaster was approaching them, but the call was loud in her ears now. The Macdonald clan was one of those she had always guarded, and her instinct told her that at this moment there was a Macdonald on a boat in Loch Linnhe. If this boat might also hold the boggarts' enemy, against whom they were taking the Nuckelavee, her

Macdonald would be in danger, and must be warned of that.

So she closed her eyes and said some words again, and took herself to the *Trout Queen*.

William Trout's large boat lay peacefully at anchor in the silent loch, with its owner deep asleep inside it. The only person aboard who was awake, so early in the morning, was David Macdonald, who was in the galley making himself a cup of tea. He treasured the hours of the day when his employer's confident voice was not in his ears. Standing there waiting for the kettle to boil, he thought again of the thing that would not now go out of his mind: his contest in verse with someone who must surely have belonged not to the human race, but to characters from the old stories, the Blue Men of the Minch. The Blue Men of the Minch, who did not exist.

David Macdonald sighed. The kettle began to whistle, and he grabbed it hastily from the stove and poured water into the teapot.

But the whistling seemed to go on. He raised his head, puzzled. It was coming from outside, and it was not a whistle but a kind of wail: long, insistent, repeated. It was eerie. He found the hair prickling on the back of his neck, as it had when he was hearing the disembodied voice over the water of the Minch. His grandmother's storytelling crept into his mind, and he knew again that in this modern world there were ancient things that he did not understand, but should respect.

His grandmother, however, had never told him about the Caointeach.

He went from the galley, through the cockpit and up onto

the deck. The wailing was much louder here; it seemed to be coming from the bow, though there was nobody to be seen there. As he crossed the deck, the wails grew shorter and swifter and louder still, rising to a scream, and he felt a wave of panic, not just at the screeching that was hurting his ears but at the fact that it would certainly wake up William Trout.

Then a last high scream broke off, and there was silence.

The Caointeach, who had been sitting invisible on the high point of the bow, wailing out her warning, saw that her Macdonald had heard it. That meant that he had been given the message that peril might be about to strike, and she knew she had done her duty. So she disappeared, and went back to the place from which she had come.

And an angry shout came from the cabin where William Trout had been asleep, and David Macdonald knew that whatever the screams might mean, he had certainly lost his peaceful moments alone with a cup of tea.

Freddy Winter, asleep in a small cabin deeper in the hull of the *Trout Queen*, was jolted awake not by the wailing of the Caointeach but by the ringing of his cell phone. He had set it to the loud, piercing ring of an old-fashioned telephone, which was useful in breaking through the noise of everyday seaboard life but earsplitting for a sleeping man in a silent room. Freddy's arm flailed about, trying to turn it off.

"Wha?" he said at last into the phone.

The voice was so excited that at first he had no idea what it was saying. It was a Scottish voice, belonging to one of the most recent watchers Freddy had hired in William Trout's urgent, determined search for sightings of the transplanted Loch Ness Monster.

"I've seen it!" cried the voice. "I've seen the Monster! I've seen the Monster, clear as can be!"

"Calm down," Freddy said. "That's great, but calm down. Tell me where you are."

"I've seen *two* monsters!" the voice shouted.

"Two?" said Freddy.

"Two! Well, the other one wasnae clear, it was under the water, but it was there, you could tell! Maybe the monster has a mate!"

Freddy paid no attention to the second half of this report, which struck him as hysterical guesswork. He said patiently, "Where are you?"

"I'm in Ledaig," said the voice. "It was heading north, toward you."

"Did you get a picture?"

"I tried, but it must have been moving too fast."

"Okay. Thanks a lot. Keep watching."

Freddy put down his phone, rolled out of bed and began pulling on his clothes.

Even without a photograph, William Trout had to be told as soon as possible that his Loch Ness Monster was still there.

Nessie was enjoying himself. He had always liked swimming in Monster shape, dropping his head and his long neck into the water and shooting along, mostly submerged, with side-to-side strokes of his great tail. He headed up through Loch Linnhe, glancing behind now and again to make sure that the

Nuckelavee was still following, trying not to go too fast for it to keep up. The creature seemed to have trouble with the Old Speech, but Nessie thought he was picking up a vague sense of pleasure from its swirling progress. Communicating with the Boggart was much easier, though he was not quite sure whether his cousin was in the air or the water.

"*Where shall we go, cuz?*" he called.

"*To the man's nasty boat!*" the Boggart called back.

"*This will scare him! Just one look at the Nuckelavee and he'll go away!*"

"*He will—and we need to have our people here, to show them. I'll fetch them. Take a wide way, don't get there till we come!*"

Nessie swooped happily down through the water and up again. "*I'll do that!*" He turned his head and tried once more to call to the monstrous swift-whirling presence behind him.

"*How do you like our sea loch, my mannie?*"

The Nuckelavee let out a gurgling underwater roar, and there was no knowing what it said, but it was still following him. Nessie swam on, heading for Shuna, a peaceful green island in the loch just north of Castle Keep and the *Trout Queen*.

And the Boggart, at high speed, headed for his people, to deliver the news.

SEVENTEEN

Granda was in the kitchen with Tom, cooking bacon again, this time for their breakfast. Portia had just arrived, though she didn't normally work on a Saturday.

"Your life seems to be a little complicated at the moment," she said. "I thought you might want to be free of the store."

"You are a good person, Portia," Angus Cameron said. He dropped slices of bread into the toaster and started fishing bacon out of the skillet.

"Breakfast, Portia?" said Tom, stealing a piece.

"I've had some. Thank you."

"Let's call up the stairs to my sleepy children."

But before they could take a step, Allie and Jay came clattering down toward them, wide awake and fully dressed. The Boggart was flittering over their heads. In a breakneck journey from the loch, he had hurtled through their open bedroom window and begun babbling to them, as fast as he could in his stumbling Scottish English.

"Granda, we have to go out in the boat!" Allie said urgently.

"The Boggart says they've got the scary Nuckelavee in the loch, to send away Mr. Trout!" said Jay. "Nessie's out there with him, showing it where to go!"

Portia, Tom and Angus stared at them.

"First I've heard of this," Granda said. He looked round the room, ending at his own window, which was also open. "Boggart?" he said reproachfully.

The Boggart made a faint buzzing sound, embarrassed. When he arrived he had been heading for Angus and Tom in the kitchen, but had changed course to the twins' window when he saw Portia arrive downstairs.

Portia said, matter-of-fact, "It's because I'm here. I'm English, I'm not connected. They have their rules—my old Welsh grannie used to say that the *pwca* wouldn't deliver really important news in front of anyone who didn't have Welsh blood."

She looked up at the ceiling. "Use the Gaelic, Boggart," she said. "I shan't understand a word."

Then they saw her pause, startled, and touch her face. A small invisible hand had brushed her cheek, and the Boggart's husky voice spoke to Granda and Tom hastily in Gaelic. It was only a few minutes before the four Camerons were headed out of the kitchen door, each clutching a piece of toast, headed for Granda's dinghy, with the Boggart flittering above their heads.

Portia watched them go. She touched her cheek again, and smiled.

Hugely excited, still in his pajamas on the deck of the yacht, William Trout said, "He saw the Monster? Where?"

"Down the coast, coming up toward us," Freddy said.

"Did he get a picture?"

"Moving too fast, he said. If it keeps on going, it should be somewhere near us in, oh, maybe fifteen minutes."

Trout instantly forgot his rage at the mysterious wails and screams that had brought him up on deck into the chilly morning air. "Somebody get my clothes!" he commanded. "And Macdonald, where are your binoculars?"

The captain turned reluctantly toward the cockpit of the *Trout Queen*, as the Trout voice rose, following him. "And pull up the anchor, start the engine, so we're ready to move! Or wait a minute, no, get Freddy's dinghy in the water, we may need to follow the thing fast!"

David Macdonald reached for a pair of binoculars and held them out. "The inflatable isnae such a great idea," he said.

"Oh yes it is," said William Trout. "Much faster than ours. And I'll take a real camera this time. Where are my pants?" He grabbed the binoculars and began peering at the coast.

"I have a good camera," Freddy said. "I'll go get it."

A crewman came scurrying with an armful of clothes. "Here, Mr. Trout!"

Trout thrust the binoculars at him and began hastily peeling off his pajamas; they were the trademark Trout black, with *WT* emblazoned in yellow on the pocket. The crewman politely turned his back until he was fully dressed.

William Trout snorted derisively, grabbing the binoculars back from him. He looked south toward Castle Keep, and suddenly he yelled, pointing.

"There's the Camerons' boat! Going after the Monster! They must have seen it too—why else would they be out so early in the morning? Crafty so-and-sos! Macdonald! Freddy! Where's that camera? Where's the boat?"

Macdonald said a few quick words to two other crewmen,

and they disappeared. Freddy came back and handed a camera to Mr. Trout. "There's a lot on there, and it's not backed up," he said. "Take care of it."

"You're coming too, you're taking me," Trout said. "Right now! We're following them!"

Freddy said in dismay, "We are?"

"For the Lord's sake, Mr. Trout," said David Macdonald, "ye're obsessed! This is foolishness! You want to risk lives for a publicity stunt?"

William Trout said, "We're going!"

Macdonald said, "If there really is some creature out there, and it's large, it's a danger to a small boat."

"Are you crazy?" said Trout. "A mega tourist attraction, that's what this is—if it's a danger, how come it's never hurt anybody in all these years? Anyway, I'm a great swimmer. A picture, that's what I want, and that's what we're going to get *right now!*"

David Macdonald looked at the naked alarm on Freddy's face. He thought again about the rhyming Blue Man of the Minch, and about his grandmother, and he knew what he should do, as a Scot and as a Macdonald. He turned toward the stern, where the dinghy was being lowered into the water.

"Freddy doesn't know these waters like I do," he said. "I'm taking you."

"Where are you, cuz?" said the Boggart. *"Where are you?"*

Granda had brought the boat out into the loch off the outer edge of Castle Keep's little island and was cruising slowly, waiting for instructions.

"*North of you,*" Nessie said, from under the water. "*Outside Shuna Island. I'll come down toward you. You'll see me—and after that I'll change. Don't worry, I'll not let the invader see me, oh no!*"

"*Is our friend happy with you?*"

"*He likes to swim—he's under the water all the time. But I've told him to come up when we reach the big boat. Just come up and show himself. Huge and horrible—this time the man'll be scared out of his wits!*"

"*We're on our way!*" the Boggart said. He flittered down through the cool morning air to hover near Granda's ear, and reported this conversation to him.

"So if we head for the big boat too," he said, "we'll see what happens when the Nuckelavee shows itself to the invading man!"

Granda pushed up the power and sent their boat along the coast of the loch, past the distant *Trout Queen*. "Is Nessie still in his monster shape?" he called, over the engine noise.

"I hope not," said Tom Cameron.

"Oh he mustn't be—that's just what Trout would love, if he saw him," Allie said, worried. "He'd want to stay, not leave."

Jay said: "She's right, he wouldn't care about anything else. *Look, I've got the Loch Ness Monster! Pay fifty pounds and I'll show him to you!*"

"No, no," the Boggart said. "Once they get near the big boat, Nessie will change shape. It's the Nuckelavee that the Trout man will see—and he'll nae want to see anything on our loch again, ever."

So Granda steered fast across the wide stretch of grey water toward Shuna Island. And they were all so intent on looking for signs of Nessie and his swirling companion that not one of them glanced back toward the *Trout Queen*, to see that a small boat was speeding after them.

It was Freddy Winter's inflatable dinghy, with David Macdonald at the tiller and William Trout in front of him. The boat bounced and bumped over the waves as they chased Granda's much slower dinghy, and big William Trout clutched a rope with one hand and Freddy's camera with the other. The binoculars swung to and fro around his neck.

Macdonald followed Granda's boat as it curved outward round the coast of Shuna Island to head back down the loch. His engine snarled when he increased the power, but the Camerons couldn't hear it above their own engine's noise. They were all peering ahead, looking for any sign of Nessie— and then Jay gave a shout.

"There he is! Look!"

For a moment, they saw the unmistakable long neck rise out of the water ahead, moving fast, the head pointing in the direction of the *Trout Queen*.

And from the boat behind them, William Trout saw it too. He shouted, ecstatic.

"It's the Monster!" he cried to Macdonald. "Ahead of them— look! I knew it! Got to get a picture—go past them, quick!"

Caught up by the sight of the creature he had thought impossible, Macdonald pushed his throttle as high as it would go, and the inflatable rose up on its side as it half-flew in a tight curve. For Granda, it seemed to come out of nowhere, suddenly whizzing past him and cutting across his bow, perilously close. He let out a yell of alarm and slowed down.

"Who the hell is that?"

"It's Trout! What's he doing here?"

"If he's not on the yacht, he won't see the Nuckelavee!"

Nessie saw and heard none of this; he had ducked below the surface again.

"All right, cuz!" he called merrily to the Boggart. *"The Nuckelavee's on his way to the big boat. I'm changing out of monster shape, and we'll follow him!"*

So he became formless and invisible again, and the Boggart dropped down into the loch to join him.

William Trout and David Macdonald were waiting for Nessie to reappear, circling above the swirl of water where they had last seen him. Trout stood up eagerly in the boat, bracing his feet against the sides, holding his camera at the ready. He was laughing with anticipation.

"I know it's here, Angus Cameron!" he yelled across the water to Granda. "You can't fool the Trout! I'm gonna get my picture! The Loch Ness Monster will be the Trout Resort Monster now!"

But beneath them now was not Nessie but the Nuckelavee. And hearing William Trout's voice, the Nuckelavee knew that the thing it most hated, a human being, was close and unprotected. Instantly, any thought of the Boggart or Nessie vanished from its mind. It forgot everything they had asked it to do, and it became entirely a ferocious, pitiless Wild Thing, with only one instinct to follow. In a great eruption of water and foam, it shot upward out of the loch, and above it the air-filled, lightweight boat spun up and sideways and almost capsized. The camera dropped into the loch as Trout and Macdonald clutched in panic at their seats.

From a distance, the Camerons watched in horror, their own boat rocking wildly.

The Nuckelavee reared up over the water, bellowing from the vast, wide-open, evil-smelling mouth of its horse's head. The great red eye glared down, and on the body towering above it, the man's head rolled from side to side very fast, grinning, to and fro, to and fro, in a frenzy of excitement. All the skinless body gleamed bright red in the daylight, moist and sticky, with the thick white muscles jumping and twisting among the yellow veins that swelled with black blood.

Gazing down, the enormous red eye and the two rolling eyes gleamed, as they saw the shiny head of William Trout.

Trout lay in the dinghy below, blinking up wide-eyed, speechless with astonishment and fear. And the creature's two long arms reached down with its skinless hands, and plucked him out of the boat.

EIGHTEEN

The Nuckelavee held William Trout high in the air for a moment, and then dropped him down onto its monstrous sticky red back. Trout shrieked in terror. The flesh clung to him as if it were coated with glue, and a great rippling white muscle pinned him against the raw chest of the half-human upper body. He was caught in a nightmare, with no way out. The grinning, sliding head above him curved out and around and came close to him, upside down, laughing. Its breath smelled of decay. William Trout tried desperately to call for help, but his throat was bone-dry from fear.

From the boat, the Camerons could see Trout struggling there, trapped, wedged among the thicket of throbbing veins and muscles where the man's torso joined the back of the horse. The Nuckelavee was swimming along the Shuna Island coast on the surface of the water, and it seemed now to be enjoying itself. A triumphant gurgling laugh came from the upper head, and its rolling speeded up.

"No!" the Boggart shrieked. "Nuckelavee! No!"

Granda broke out of the frozen horror that had hold of them all, and struggled to turn the boat into the waves still rocking it.

Behind them they saw David Macdonald, white-faced, frantically baling water out of the dinghy.

William Trout let out a terrible wordless howl.

Jay said, appalled, "What can we do?"

"He was supposed to just *see* it, from the big boat!" Allie said.

Granda said, teeth clenched, fighting his steering wheel, "He came out to chase Nessie, for a publicity picture, I bet. *Stupid* man!"

"*Stop, Nuckelavee!*" the Boggart yelled, and the Nuckelavee paid no attention, and laughed, and swam. It was all wild instinct, and it was preparing to dive, to drown William Trout.

"Help me!" Trout screamed. "Help!"

Desperately, Nessie changed back into the shape of the Monster and shot up out of the water nearby. The Nuckelavee looked at him, paused, and laughed again, proudly.

Suddenly Allie remembered the MacDevon's book, and its Gaelic monsters.

"Fresh water!" she shrieked. "The one thing that can stop it—the book said! Fresh water!"

Granda's memory jabbed at him too. "Come here," he yelled to Jay. "This little door—there's a bottle of water—"

Jay lurched past him, found the door below the steering-wheel console, opened it, and reached for a plastic bottle, half-full of water, rolling among an anchor and coils of rope and chain. Hastily he pulled off its cap and thrust the bottle into Allie's outstretched hand, as Granda fought to come closer to the speeding Nuckelavee. She swung her arm to spray the water from the bottle at the huge red body as it passed—but the wind blew the water straight back at them.

On his way after the Nuckelavee and the writhing William Trout, Nessie drew level with the dinghy, towering over them.

"Nessie!" Tom Cameron clung to the side of the tossing boat and waved one hand frantically, pointing ahead. "Nessie! Get it to Shuna! There's a stream—just over there—"

Nessie swam faster and bent his long neck over the Nuckelavee, making a strange, gentle hissing sound. He swam round it in a swift circle, turning it toward the island as Granda managed to send his boat frothing closer to the shore. Ahead, they could see a break in the shoreline, a little estuary, where a spring emptied out into the salty water of the loch.

"Yes!" Allie said. "Oh yes!"

And suddenly it was as if all their minds were touching, working together without thought, like the shifting cloud of birds that swoops and weaves its way through an autumn sky. For a few moments, as the Nuckelavee swam unwittingly on, Nessie and Granda's boat were at either side of it like sheepdogs, gently heading it toward the dwindling current of spring water flowing into the loch.

And then, just for a moment or two, they were crossing the current, its water streaming around them. Only a little of the fresh water touched the Nuckelavee's huge body, only a very little—but it was enough.

The Nuckelavee gave a dreadful scream, and it swung outward to escape, rearing up so suddenly that a great wave leaped out around it, making the Camerons' boat toss wildly once more. And William Trout fell from the creature's back and splashed into the water. He was the only one who heard the angry sucking sound that came from the skinless body as it had to let him go, and he would never forget it as long as he lived.

He came up to the surface, gasping, dropped down and came up again, clutching in panic for the side of the boat. Granda threw the motor into neutral to stop the whirling propeller from cutting him, and fought the waves to hold the boat still enough for the others to grab him and pull him aboard. Because Trout was so big a man, this was not easy, and one side tipped perilously low. The strap of his binoculars caught on a cleat, trapping him, and Tom ripped it off his neck; the binoculars sank even faster than the camera had gone.

The Nuckelavee screamed again, in rage as well as pain, and it disappeared, diving deep into the loch. So did Nessie, diving after it, with the Boggart following.

William Trout tumbled into the bottom of the boat, sobbing with terror and relief, gasping out sounds that were not quite words. Tom Cameron grabbed him, turning his head sideways, but although he was coughing up water, he could still breathe. "No . . . no . . . ," he was spluttering. "No . . . no . . ."

"It's all right," Tom said. "It's all right. You're safe. It's gone."

Granda had the motor barely running now; the boat rocked, but gradually less as the waves calmed down.

Trout was still babbling, his face twisted with fear. "Came for me!" he kept gasping. "It came for me!"

"You're all right—you're safe!" Tom said again. He helped the big man roll over, and propped him up against the side of the boat; Trout's arms and legs were jerking strangely. He lay there wide-eyed, fearful, staring out at the loch.

"It came for me!" he said. "Got to get away! Get away!" He moaned, as if he were going to cry.

Tom looked across at his father and nodded, and Granda headed the boat slowly toward the edge of Shuna Island. As they came round the coast they could see the *Trout Queen*, out across the water on the way to Castle Keep. Granda pushed the throttle, and the boat began to bump faster over the waves. Behind them came the other dinghy; David Macdonald had managed to restart his motor, and he was following.

Allie was staring out across the loch. "That thing, that awful thing! Where did it go?"

"The boggarts have it," Granda shouted, above the noise. "Don't worry—they're in charge!"

"It was *disgusting!*"

"Aye, well, that was their idea—he'd see something so terrible that he'd go away. Nobody expected him to put his boat on top of it." Angus Cameron glanced at Tom and the retching wet wreck that was William Trout, and slowed the boat down a little.

"What if Allie hadn't remembered about the fresh water?" Jay said.

His grandfather said, "Best not tae think about that."

William Trout was sitting hunched in the stern, shaking, but he was breathing more normally again. As the naked terror faded out of his face and he began to think again, he had become very quiet. He glanced nervously out at the loch from time to time, but he avoided catching the eye of anyone in the boat, even Tom Cameron, who was right beside him. It was as if he was pretending that they weren't there.

The *Trout Queen* was looming ahead of them, its massive bulk barely moving in the choppy water. When they reached its tall white side, Trout tried to get to his feet, but Tom had to help him up, standing swaying beside him to keep him from falling down.

"Thank you," Trout muttered as the twins clutched the yacht's broad stern platform, holding their boat close so he could climb out. "Thank you." He reached an arm to the outstretched hands of a waiting sailor.

David Macdonald brought the inflatable dinghy up beside Granda's boat, and Granda reached out to hold it steady, in the small waves bouncing them both up and down against the big boat's side. Macdonald got to his feet, balancing on his long legs, and jumped nimbly onto the *Trout Queen*'s platform, holding his boat's bow line. He and Granda looked at each other. Watching their faces, Allie thought: *it's like they're talking in their minds—I wonder what they're saying?*

"*Mòran taing*, Angus," David Macdonald said.

"'*S e do bheatha*, David," said Granda.

Above them, on the big boat, Freddy Winter came hurrying into the group of sailors as they helped the dripping William Trout aboard.

"What happened?" he demanded.

William Trout said hoarsely, "I fell in."

"A hot bath and warm clothes," Granda called.

"Yes," said William Trout. He glanced at David Macdonald as he came onto the deck, and then looked away.

"But what *happened*?" said Freddy.

"That's all!" William Trout snapped. "I fell in the water! End of story!"

He glared at Freddy and shrugged off a sailor who was trying to steady him on the slanting deck. Then he stumbled into the warm, welcoming interior of his yacht, where a steward had already scurried to his bathroom to run hot water into the shiny white tub with the gold-plated taps.

"Did you see the Monster?" Freddy said eagerly to Macdonald.

The captain looked out at Granda, who was turning his boat away from the *Trout Queen* as the twins pushed it off. He raised a hand to him and glanced back at Freddy, expressionless. "You'll have to ask your Mr. Trout," he said.

"He didn't want to tell them!" Jay said, baffled, as Granda headed the boat back toward Castle Keep and home. "A story like an amazing horror movie, and he didn't want to tell them!"

"I think you'll find he won't talk to us about it either," Tom Cameron said.

"Why?" said Allie.

"He was terrified," said their father. "And no wonder. But that's not part of his image. Nobody, nothing frightens William Trout—he's in control. He's the boss."

"Nobody but us saw him scared to death," Granda said.

"Us and David Macdonald. Tom's right—Trout wants to keep it that way."

"Does that mean the Boggart's plan hasn't worked?" Allie said.

"I think it's worked fine," Granda said. "Just you wait and see."

David Macdonald waited for an hour, and then he went below and knocked on the door of William Trout's cabin.

"Mr. Trout?" he called. "It's David Macdonald."

There was a short pause, and then Trout opened the door. He was muffled in a bathrobe and clutching a blanket round his shoulders. "Come in," he said.

"I just wanted to make sure ye were all right," Macdonald said. He shut the door behind him.

"You're a discreet man," Trout said. "I take it you haven't spoken to anyone about what happened."

"I doubt they would have believed me," Macdonald said. "I'm no' sure I believe it myself. Even after the Minch." He peered at Trout. "*Are* ye all right?"

"Yes," said Trout. His shoulder gave a strange upward jerk, and he pulled his blanket back around it. Then he sat down suddenly on his bed. For a moment, his voice lost its usual confident bounce.

"You're a Scot," he said. "Have you ever seen things like this before?"

"No," said David Macdonald. "But I've heard tell o' them. This is an old, old country."

Trout gave his bald head a quick shake, as if he could shake away the memories. He said, more confident again, "I'd be grateful if you'd sign a document promising you'll make no disclosure of what we saw today. None at all."

David Macdonald said, "Are ye joking?"

William Trout stared at him. "Of course not."

"I give ye my word, willingly," Macdonald said coldly. "So there is no need for a signature."

"I'm a businessman, Macdonald," Trout said. He gave a small patient sigh, like a teacher faced with a totally ignorant student.

Macdonald said, "And I'm a Scot, and I keep my word. If ye had more than a trickle o' Scots blood in your veins, ye'd know that. But ye do have a trickle, I understand, so I'll not take offense at the insult. *Théid dúthchas an aghaidh nan creag.*"

"Whatever that may mean," William Trout said.

"Kinship will withstand the rocks," said David Macdonald. "Though I can think of others I'd rather be kin to." He moved to the door, and looked back before he turned the handle. "I will steer your ship for as long as it takes for you to find a new captain, Mr. Trout," he said. "But I ask you to look for one."

Trout sighed again. "What are we paying you?" he said. "I'll give you a raise."

"It wouldn't be enough," David Macdonald said.

The Nuckelavee churned its way across the loch, underwater, grunting with pain and rage, and at intervals letting out a great angry roar. The Boggart and Nessie slid invisibly along on either side of it, trying to make soothing sounds, trying to calm its wild magic with the patience of Old Things. As they neared the Seal Rocks, they saw the seals underwater, weaving up and down and side to side, puzzled by the emotion that they could feel through the water around them. Like all sea creatures, seals see more strange sights than most creatures who live their lives on land, and they were troubled not by the Nuckelavee's hideous appearance but by its distress.

The Boggart, who all his life had sung only warlike songs, even tried to croon the Nuckelavee a lullaby as he swam.

"Baloo baleeerie, baloo baleerie," he sang in his husky half-heard voice. *"Baloo baleerie, baloo balee . . ."*

And very gradually, the awful Nuckelavee began to calm down. It swam more slowly; it grew quiet, and the head of the human-looking part of its body stopped whipping from side to side quite so fast. The seals began diving around it, cautiously, swooping to and fro at a distance, and it seemed to find them comforting. It even spoke to the boggarts, using the Old Speech.

"There are seals at my home too," it said in its toneless, rusty voice. *"But not so many as there used to be. I like your seals. I like your seals."*

"So do we," Nessie said, and he swam, invisibly but companionably, around the Nuckelavee's two heads. He wanted very much to shape-shift into a seal himself, but he suspected the Nuckelavee didn't know the complicated habits of boggarts and might be confused.

"We'll keep the Nuckelavee calm tonight," the Boggart said. *"And tomorrow I will go to our people, to see what happened to the invader when he fell in the loch."*

"Whatever it was," Nessie said, *"he deserved it."*

* * *

In the private dining-room of the Trout Queen that night, Trout and Freddy Winter sat down at a gleaming mahogany table. Freddy eyed his employer carefully. William Trout still looked pale and shaken, and considering that he appeared to have been half drowned earlier in the day, Freddy was amazed to have been invited to dinner. But clearly there had been some result to Trout's passionate search for the Loch Ness Monster, and he was itching to hear what it was.

The steward served them both their first course, steaming bowls of mushroom soup made, he reported confidentially, from mushrooms picked that morning in an Argyll meadow. He filled their wineglasses with wine, their water glasses with Scottish sparkling water. Then he turned to go. Freddy could see Mr. Trout watching until he had left the room.

Trout said, "I'm tired of this hunt for the Loch Ness Monster, Freddy. You can give it up."

"Oh," Freddy said cautiously. "Okay." He sipped his soup.

William Trout's left shoulder gave a sudden twitch, jerking upward. "I don't think people would find it an attraction," he said. "Wrong decision. I very seldom make mistakes, but that was one."

"Whatever you say, boss," Freddy said.

Trout said, "I'm having a no-disclosure document drawn up, for you and the two guys who saw what we saw, that day. And the spotter on the loch, too. Everyone will guarantee they'll never talk about it—not online, or to the press, or to anyone. You'd have no trouble signing that, I'm sure."

"Of course not," Freddy said.

Trout looked at his plate without appetite. "It's a strange place, this," he said. "You hear stories that are very hard to believe."

"Very hard," Freddy said.

"I don't believe in passing on stories like that, do you?"

"Absolutely not," said Freddy. "This soup is excellent."

Okay, he thought to himself. *So we don't talk about the Monster, not even to each other. And we'll never know what happened to him today.*

"Tell me," said Trout, "how far precisely have we come with this project, as of today? What's the progress report?"

Freddy drank some more soup. "The little castle jetty's finished," he said, "and the big one's half-done. We start dredging for the marina next week. The farm has gone, the berm facing the Camerons is done, so long as you think it's high enough. We can start the hotel foundation as soon as Mr. Tutti sends the revised plans."

"Very good," said William Trout. His shoulder jerked upward again, and he grabbed crossly at his left arm to stop it. "Are you enjoying Scotland, Freddy?"

"Not much, to be honest," Freddy said. He added hastily, "But hey, I love my job. Some places are just better than others."

"Ah," said Trout. He sipped some sparkling water. "It's not public knowledge yet," he said, "but I'm about to build a new resort, probably in Ireland. I plan on sending you over there to head up the project."

"Wow!" Freddy said.

"With a major salary increase, of course."

Freddy beamed. "That's terrific."

"Not a word to the press yet, though," said William Trout. He tried hard to smile at Freddy, as the steward appeared in the doorway with their next course. "I'm still working on it."

"You bet, boss," said Freddy Winter. "And just give us that paper to sign when you're ready, me and the other guys. They'll be going to Ireland too, right? And maybe with a raise?"

"Of course," Trout said.

Freddy said, "Great!"

He watched with interest as his employer's shoulder gave another uncontrollable upward twitch.

NINETEEN

To the twins' surprise and delight, Granda put everyone—including Portia—back into the boat next day and announced that they were going to Castle Keep.

"We don't have permission," Allie said.

"Nor did you," said Granda. "And I want to see those plans of his for myself, just in case we need them."

They took the rest of Allie's chocolate chip cookies, in a tin, and other things for a teatime picnic. As they climbed up the rocky approach to Castle Keep, on its little island, there was no knowing whether it was the cookies or the castle that brought the Boggart to join them.

A breeze blew round their heads, though the day was calm, and faintly they heard a husky voice humming the tune of "Hey Johnnie Cope."

"Boggart!" said Jay.

The Boggart said from the air, "The invading man has caught a cold."

"Good!" said Tom Cameron. "And where is the terrible Nuckelavee?"

"He is calm," the Boggart said. "And swimming with Nessie,

and the seals." He dived in through the doorway, as Granda opened the castle door with the heavy iron key. He was humming again; from the kitchen they could hear faint snatches of the tune come and go as he flew round all the passages and rooms of the castle, inspecting it.

"He sounds cheerful," Allie said. "But how do we know if his plan worked? Even after yesterday, we don't know what Trout will do."

"You never can tell wi' boggarts," Granda said. "They show what's blowin', they're like weather vanes. Maybe he's had a lurk round the yacht and heard things that we don't know. Come on—the library."

Portia was filling the kettle. "I'll catch you up," she said. "I'm making tea."

Jay and Allie led the little procession down the passage and up the stairs. Now that they were looking in daylight, they could see that the stone walls of the corridor were lined with bright pictures of Trout resorts in other countries: a hotel in the Bahamas, a casino in South America, a golf course in Ireland.

But in the library, all the signs of Trout occupation had gone away. The tables had been moved back to their original places, and the MacDevon's big oak desk was back where it had been. All the files and papers had been taken away, and there was no sign of the two models of the Trout Castle Resort. The few parts of the walls that were not covered by bookshelves held only dark prints of Highland landscapes, as they always had.

"Everything's gone!" Allie said, disappointed. "They must have come over this morning."

"Never mind," said Granda. "We have your pictures."

Tom Cameron said, "And I have a feeling Dad's right—we may not need them again."

They heard a faint whistling in the air; it was the tune of "Hey Johnnie Cope" again.

Allie looked round at the book-lined walls. "Where are you, Boggart?" she said.

The Boggart said, "He's come, in a wee boat! He's here!" His voice faded away, as he darted into his favorite resting place on the high shelf.

"Who's here?"

Portia came carefully through the door carrying a tray loaded with teacups, sugar bowl, milk jug. Behind her, carrying the teapot, came William Trout. He was dressed all in black. His bald head gleamed, and his nose was rather red.

"You have a visitor," Portia said. "If 'visitor' is the right word."

"We're the visitors," Granda said. He gave Trout a cold, unsmiling look, but moved aside so that he could put the teapot on a desk. Trout just managed to set it down before giving an enormous sneeze, clapping his free hand to his face.

"Excuse me," he said through the hand. He pulled a fistful of tissues from his pocket and blew his nose.

"You caught cold," Portia said brightly, reaching for the teapot. "Not surprising, I suppose." She poured tea and began handing round the cups, along with Allie's tin of cookies.

William Trout looked at her more closely, with caution. "You heard that I fell in the loch, I guess." His left shoulder jerked upward, and his face flickered with irritation.

Granda said, "She knows why, too. Portia is part of the

family." He sat down in a big armchair, with his cup of tea.

"Oh," said William Trout. "Well."

He drew himself upright, standing there in his black Trout Corporation jacket with a thick black turtleneck underneath, and he took the teacup Portia handed him and put it down on the nearest bookshelf. They gazed at him, seeing in their minds the shrieking figure stuck captive on the skinless red back of the Nuckelavee, the sodden, terrified wreck of a man gibbering in the bottom of a rocking dinghy.

Trout turned to Granda. "I saw you all coming to the castle, and I decided we should have a talk," he said. "About yesterday."

"Talk away," Granda said.

"First, I have to thank you all for your help," Trout said. He paused, and stood looking at them, as if he were waiting for something.

They looked back, expressionless.

"You're welcome," Tom Cameron said.

William Trout inclined his head graciously. "Then . . . clearly there are things about this place that I didn't know when I chose it." He sounded stiff and formal, as if he were addressing a public meeting. "As you must know, I have a fiduciary responsibility to the guests who come to stay at my resorts. Their safety is in my hands, as well as their enjoyment. Now that I've found out there are highly dangerous creatures in Loch Linnhe, in all conscience I can't expose anyone to that danger."

Allie clutched Jay's arm, silently, hopefully.

"Quite right," Tom Cameron said. He nodded his head very

slowly and soberly at William Trout. "Quite right—you could get sued for very large sums of money," he said.

"You could indeed," said Granda gravely. "You might be in trouble if anyone even *saw* a dangerous creature, let alone got attacked by one."

Jay burst out, "So are you going away?"

William Trout ignored him, but suddenly his stiffness was gone. "Where did you find that obscene animal?" he said to Granda. "And how do you control it?"

"We don't," Granda said.

"Of course you do!" Trout said. "That's why it came for me!" His left shoulder gave a great twitch again, and he clutched at it. "Came for me . . . ," he said, muffled.

"I would have been scared too," said Allie. "It was an awful, awful thing, I was terrified just looking at it."

Mr. Trout gave a forced little laugh. He let go of his shoulder and picked up his teacup. "Nothing scares the Trout," he said. "I am one of the bravest people you will ever meet!"

Then he sneezed. "Shoot!" he said, and blew his nose.

"I could have sworn that was a frightened man we pulled out of the water," Tom Cameron said. "Frightened out of his wits. Babbling."

William Trout opened his mouth for an angry retort, and then closed it again. He glared at Tom. "Listen, Cameron," he said. "I'm a very smart businessman, and one of the reasons I'm so good is that I know when to walk away from a deal. Even if it costs me. I don't know how you people have control over that appalling creature, but I do know I'm going to make very sure I never get near it again. Ever."

"Mr. Trout?" Granda said. He got up out of his chair and stood facing the big man. His mop of white hair looked even wilder than usual.

"Gi'e a thought, Mr. Trout, to a place where no man has control," he said softly. "A place with wild things, that no man can buy, or own, or use. This place doesnae want ye, Mr. Trout. Nor all your concrete and towers and dirt, wi' your high talk about jobs that means nothing but a way to make you money. This place wants ye to go."

"Well, I'm going!" William Trout said furiously. "I've never liked this country—tight little place with its secret language—no wonder my grandmother left! I'm getting my resort out of here and I'm never coming back." He drew himself up and pointed a finger at Granda. "Just don't think that means that you can control the Trout, you or anyone else! The heck with this creepy Scottish loch—I can do anything I want, anywhere in the world!"

He glared at them all, eyes wide—and then suddenly he swatted at the top of his bald head. "Damn it," he said, "the place still has bugs!"

The Boggart, having emerged to help himself to a cookie, had turned himself into a fly once more. Giggling, he made a second dive at William Trout, and Trout swatted again and succeeded only in smacking his own skull.

He glanced down at his teacup and handed it to Portia. Then he looked round at the Camerons, without meeting anyone's eye.

"I'll be in touch," he said. "We hope to have a press conference in a few days' time." And he turned and left the room.

Jay let out a whoop, and Portia and Tom Cameron joined in. Allie gave her grandfather a joyous hug.

"Boggart," she said to the air, "where are you? You made it work! He's leaving, you've saved the loch!"

The fly buzzed gaily round her head, and then vanished, and they heard the Boggart giggle again.

"The invading man makes a lot o' noise about new things," he said, "but this is where the Old Things live."

Ewan Nicolson was on duty for William Trout's new press conference, which was held on the land between Granda's store and the jetty. There was very little grass left on the dirt, but most of the trucks and bulldozers were gone. The announcement that the Trout Corporation had put out on the Internet about their change of plan was so unexpected, and so brief, that there were far more cameras and reporters than there had been the first time, even without large Trout buses to bring them in.

Voices buzzed, cars were crammed into the parking lot surrounding Freddy's Site Office, and in the store, Portia did a brisk trade in snacks and cold drinks. Granda, Tom and the twins sat behind the closed kitchen door, waiting for the press conference to begin and listening to Portia's varied and creative ways of telling all eager press inquirers that they weren't there.

Ewan sat in his car, watching all the arrivals. It was late morning; the sky was overcast but the breeze was gentle, and his car window was open. Suddenly something was filling it, and he glanced up to see David Macdonald looking in.

"David!"

"*Ciamar a tha thu?*" said David Macdonald.

"I'm fine. What's this all about, do you know?"

"Don't you?"

"I'm just a policeman," said Ewan. "Nobody tells me anything."

Macdonald grinned. "They don't tell me much either—but I think he's packing it in."

"He *is*?" said Ewan, trying not to sound delighted. "Why?"

"Well," said David Macdonald, and he looked round at the blue-grey hills and the small waves on the loch, and the square outline of Castle Keep. He thought about the Blue Men of the Minch, about the strange shrieks he had heard onboard the *Trout Queen*, and most of all he thought about the Nuckelavee. He thought: *but Ewan doesn't know about all that, of course.*

"I think the place didn't want him," he said.

And Ewan thought about two bunches of marker flags traveling unsupported through the air, and the sound of voices ringing out over the water, joined by the plaintive wail of bagpipes that were not there. He thought: *but David doesn't know about all that, of course.*

He said, "I think you're right."

"Well," said Macdonald, "I just brought him over from the boat, so pretty soon we'll find out."

And from behind the hill of dirt that now loomed near Granda's store, there was once more the discordant little groan that heralds a real set of bagpipes beginning to play, and out came the bagpiper in his kilt and after him William Trout, in the middle of a small group of men. One of them was chunky

Freddy Winter; like the rest, he wore his trademark black Trout jacket with the bold yellow *T* on its back. But Mr. Trout was dressed very formally this time, in a dark suit, white shirt, and red tie; with his escort, he made his way to a little platform that had been put up close to the jetty, with several microphones at its inner edge.

The crowd of reporters hurried to join the cameramen, who had already planted their cameras to face the platform, and Granda, Tom, Jay and Allie emerged unnoticed from the store to join them. Mr. Trout marched slowly through their ranks, while the piper played "The Skye Boat Song." His arrival at the microphones gave the reporters a view of him set neatly against the backdrop of Castle Keep and the loch. The cameras clicked and hummed.

William Trout raised a finger to the bagpiper, and he stopped playing.

"Thank you all for coming," said Mr. Trout into the microphones. His voice was hoarse, muffled by his cold. "I've been very grateful to the people of Scotland for all their tremendous support. I have some sad news to announce, I'm afraid. Sad, sad news. In spite of the fact that my Trout Castle Resort would have brought huge benefits to the Scottish economy, not to mention hundreds of jobs for the people of Argyll, we won't be able to go ahead with it."

He paused, looking out gravely at them all. His left shoulder suddenly gave an enormous twitch. The reporters paid no attention; they were all scribbling busily in their notebooks and laptops.

"Hooray!" said Jay under his breath.

"The reason is Scottish," said Mr. Trout. "More than any-thing, we respect the nature and integrity of the landscape of Argyll and of Loch Linnhe, and the need to keep it intact. Yes indeed. I'm famous for my concern for the environment."

He looked round, facing into the cameras, nodding his head. "We all know how important it is not to disturb endangered species of plants," he said solemnly. "It has been reported to me that on the land where the Trout Castle Resort would stand, there are three—not just one, but *three*—endangered species growing, and it's unthinkable that we should disturb them. So . . ." He paused, and sighed. "We will have to take our resort elsewhere."

A reporter called, "What are the three species, Mr. Trout?"

"I didn't bring my notes with me," said William Trout. "We'll post the names on our website."

On the edge of the crowd, Granda looked down at the twins and grinned. "Plants, eh?" he said quietly. "Very, very rare plants."

Allie grinned back. "So rare they don't have names," she said.

A deep voice called, "Mr. Trout, was it the many local people opposing your development who challenged you about these plants?"

"I haven't heard anyone opposing, and I told you, we heard about them from experts," Trout said crossly.

"Who are your experts, Mr. Trout?" called the first reporter.

"I don't have their names with me," Trout said. "We'll post those on our website too. They're very, very well respected, world-famous among environmentalists."

"If you're so concerned about the environment," said the

deep voice, "why didn't you know about these plants before?"

William Trout took a deep breath and looked up at the sky. "Isn't it a beautiful day?" he said. "Such a beautiful place, I'm so, so sorry to have to leave it. In answer to your question, sir, our environmental scientists did an immensely thorough survey of this area, but they failed to notice these plants. Everyone makes a mistake now and then."

"Can't you build around the plants?" called another voice.

William Trout looked shocked. "Certainly not!" he said. "This is their habitat! You might say"—and he shook his head with a sad little smile—"they beat me. They got here first! Nobody beats the Trout, but three little plants managed it!"

His left shoulder gave a massive twitch, and his smile disappeared.

"Surely they aren't going to believe all this!" said Tom in his father's ear.

Granda said softly, "Mr. Trout is an inventive man."

A woman's voice called, "If ye're leavin', what about the damage ye've done tae our coastline?"

William Trout ran his hand over his shining head. "A restored area will be my gift to the people of Argyll and Bute. The dirt hill over there, the berm, that was created to protect the view of Mr. Angus Cameron—"

"What!" said Jay indignantly. "It was the opposite!"

"Hush," said his father, "don't confuse him with facts."

"—that berm will be demolished to create a gentle slope, as an area of public parkland. A charitable donation."

"Does this include your whole acreage?" demanded the voice.

"No, no," said Mr. Trout swiftly. "The farm fields will be sold or rented, and farmed, as they should be. And"—he raised a hand dramatically—"this enlarged jetty behind me, which would have been the basis for a state-of-the-art marina, will be left for the owners of Castle Keep."

Tom said in Granda's ear, "As compensation for the money he now won't pay to buy the place."

"So where will you build the new resort now?" called the deep voice. "Will it still be in Scotland?"

"No!" said William Trout very fast. *Get away from Scotland,* said his mind to him, loudly, insistently. *Got to get away from that Thing, and never come back.* He swallowed, and took a deep breath. "We're in the process of buying one of the sites we looked at before we came here," he said. "It's in Ireland, near Curracloe Beach in Wexford. Beautiful beaches, and wonderful views. A beautiful unspoiled place."

"And will you have local support there?"

"Of course!" said Mr. Trout crossly. "I'm leaving tomorrow to go there, to Ireland, and I expect to have a great reception. Everyone knows the Trout Corporation is good for business."

"But a massive petition has been circulating here in Argyll in opposition to your resort," the deep voice said. "My paper's had hundreds o' calls an' letters!"

"So have we!" shouted another, and a confusion of voices began calling out.

"Let's go home before we get into the news," Granda said quietly, and they backed out of the crowd and managed to reach the store before anybody noticed them.

"D'you think the Boggart was there?" Allie said.

"Maybe," Granda said. "Or maybe he and Nessie are over by the rocks having a good time with the seals."

"What about the Nuckelavee?" said Jay.

His father said, "Mr. Trout must be hoping very much that it's gone back to wherever it came from."

"I do too," Allie said.

TWENTY

But the Nuckelavee was still in Loch Linnhe—living under the water, as all sea creatures do. Nobody saw it, except the boggarts and the seals, and the unfortunate fish that it sometimes ate. Though it was clearly a very Wild Thing and spoke to the Boggart and Nessie only in short bursts, and at long intervals, they felt that it regarded them not perhaps as friends, but at least as non-enemies. Mr. Trout's boat had left the loch very soon after the press conference, but the Nuckelavee remained. It enjoyed swimming with the seals, and now understood that its two boggart companions were quite often swimming there too in the shape of seals, even though most of the time they were no more than voices, invisible.

And the Boggart was in seal shape on the day that Allie and Jay came to the Seal Rocks with their father to say good-bye. Clouds hung low over the loch but the wind was light, and Tom brought the boat close to the rocks. A curious herring gull swooped overhead, keening. As they bobbed there, a head rose from the water nearby, looking at them; they could see the whiskers and the round dark eyes, though not the very faint silver tinge of the skin that told the other seals that this was a boggart.

They heard his voice in the air, as always, not from his seal mouth.

"*Nessie's away over there with the Nuckelavee,*" he said. "*Keeping it calm. The fellow's not safe near people, you know that.*"

"We have to go back home to Canada, Boggart," Allie said. She sniffed. "We'll miss you. We came to say good-bye. And thank you."

"*Aye,*" said the Boggart, for whom time and distance did not mean as much as they do to us.

"We 're coming back next year," Jay said.

Tom Cameron said, "Tell Nessie thank you as well, Boggart."

The seal's head ducked below the water and did not come up again, and each of them in turn felt on one cheek the soft touch that was the brush of a boggart's hand. The husky voice came out of the air once more.

"*We're going on a wee trip, Nessie and me,*" the Boggart said. "*To Ireland. To a place near Curracloe Beach in Wexford, with beautiful beaches and wonderful views. A beautiful unspoiled place, which should remain unspoiled.*"

His voice began to fade, as he flittered away.

He said, "*We're taking the Nuckelavee.*"

AFTERWORD

Scotland's Loch Linnhe is indeed as beautiful as this book shows it to be, but I apologize once more to the inhabitants of Port Appin for changing its geography, and to the owners of Castle Stalker for turning it into Castle Keep. My thanks to Sìm Innes for his advice on Gaelic.

The creatures called up for the Boggart I did not invent; they're part of Scottish legend, as documented by the wonderful folklorist Katharine Briggs, and you can hear their names pronounced at http://learngaelic.net. The Blue Men of the Minch were believed to cause frequent storms around the Shiant Islands, where they lived underwater and preyed on passing ships; one theory held that they were "based on the Moorish captives called 'Blue Men' who were marooned in Ireland in the ninth century by Norwegian pirates." And the Each-Uisge (pronounced *ech-ooshga*, with the *ch* as in *loch*) is the most alarming of many legendary Highland water horses, haunting the sea and lochs.

As for the horrifying Nuckelavee, "he came out of the sea," says Ms. Briggs, "and spread evil wherever he went, blighting crops, destroying livestock and killing every man whom he could encounter." He is even nastier in legend than he is in my book. And the Caointeach (pronounced *kane-chuch*, with the first *ch* as in *chat* and the second as in *loch*) who calls up these creatures is an Argyll version of the Highland banshee; her name means "wailer," though unlike the banshee she does not, in my story, have "no nose and just one monstrous tooth."

She does love bacon, though. I'm the only person who knows that. This is one of the special pleasures of being an author who writes fantasy.